Tom,

Seek in
All things...

Jerry Weller
11/14/23

VALIS

VALIS

Jerry Welborn

Imaginal Free Press
College Grove, TN

ISBN: 9798432039187

Cover photograph by: Jerry Welborn
Printed in the United States of America

DEDICATION

This book is dedicated to my daughter, Sarah, and her husband, Jacob. They are the ones who introduced me and my wife to their friends and the enchantment of Mt. Shasta, California.

DEDICATION

This book is also in memory of the late Jay Frankenberger, a gifted Intuitive we met along the way.

DEDICATION

Jay Frankenberger

CONTENTS

CONTENTS

CHAPTER 1

On THE ROAD

It was about four o'clock that afternoon when Raymond Leonard Peters turned onto the Monteocha Road just outside of Gainesville, Florida. He passed a huge raceway on the right side of the road looking for an out-of-the-way place to park his camper for the night. Coming to an unmarked road, he turned left and drove back into a winding wooded area where he soon came to a gate. From the driver's seat, he could see that the gate appeared to be unlocked. After opening and closing the gate, he proceeded on until he reached a cul-de-sac, circled it and came to a halt. Leonard stepped out of his late model pickup. He looked around at the small clearing, took a piss, and walked back where he entered the camper to bunk down for the night.

Leonard flopped down on his bed and quickly went to sleep. When he opened his eyes, he could see a flicker of light from the front window of his camper. He got up, looked out, and could see what looked like a man feeding a campfire. Leonard withdrew a 308 pistol from a nearby drawer and tucked it under his belt. He opened the door, then addressed the stranger, "What's going on here?"

"Oh, there you are," said the stranger. "I've been waiting for you. Just one thing though, your pistol won't kill me; I'm a unified copy of a divine image. Don't be afraid. Come over and join me."

"Unified my ass; I'm dreaming."

Leonard stepped out of the camper and walked toward the stranger. He withdrew his pistol and pointed it toward the stranger in a defensive gesture. Suddenly and unexpectedly a shot rang out; Leonard could see a hole being ripped through the stranger's chest. The stranger smiled, "See, you can't kill me with a gunshot, but fear not because I'm here to help you. Come, let's sit down by the firelight and have a chat."

The two took a place across from one another with the fire flickering between them. Leonard looked over at the stranger who had long dark hair, no shirt, and wore buckskin britches. He saw an aura surrounding the stranger's body and asked, "Am I dreaming?"

"Yes and no," replied the stranger. "You're somewhere between being asleep and awake. Your experience is vivid, like it's really happening, and it really is happening; you are having an out-of-the-body experience. You see my aura, but there is a layer beyond my aura; it is my Merkabah body. Look closely, and you will see an outer layer of white light. It is through this subtle body that I am able to reach out to you. I am mediating between the third and fourth dimensions."

"You don't look like an angel or a prophet; you look Native American," said Leonard, stuttering as he spoke. "Who are you? Where do you come from?"

"Whatever I tell you, you won't believe until you reach another level of consciousness, and that is why I am here. So, let me be brief. I am appearing to you from a past life in Florida. In the early 1800s I incarnated as a Seminole Indian. My name was Monteocha. Currently, I have ascended from the Earth Star Chakra to assist in your spiritual development.

You must be in harmonic balance with the earth before moving ahead in your development. Currently, you are lost in a fog of density; you are weighted down by low frequency matter."

"What? That's nuts! I've got to be dreaming. How could you possibly know that?"

"Simple, I read your frequency, and I have answered your call. Nothing comes back empty."

"I don't remember having tried to summon the dead."

Monteocha laughed. "It doesn't work that way. It's about your being ready to take another step in your personal development. Right now, you are so dense that you don't believe in your own soul, much less that the soul is immortal. You can't hide how you emote to the universe; it calls out in a tonal frequency. Try to be honest; don't fool yourself, Leonard."

"So, what is my problem?" replied Leonard, hesitating in thought. "I should feel happy because the spool of fate has handed me a jackpot. And still, I am haunted with a blackness that wraps me like a dark storm cloud."

"So, answer the question. What is 'the Leonard issue'?" Get to the heart of it."

"I feel shaky. My problem is with words, yes words, and the sense of unsteadiness. It's like I've reached the end of my vocabulary and need some transition to get to the other side of the quandary. I've never had a problem with meaning or justifying my beliefs and actions, which is why I can no longer justify having played my part in using social media to trick the public into buying GameStop as hedge fund managers were shorting it. At one time, I might have used a cliché: 'It's a dog-eat-dog world, screw those greedy bastards.' I have an enduring doubt that my limited vocabulary can justify anything: my hopes, my fears, my dreams. And, if you want to know the truth, I don't believe that my vocabulary is any closer to the truth than the vocabulary

3

of anyone else. I remember a time when others could puncture my vocabulary or, as they say, burst my bubble. I took the wound very seriously. Now, I seem to lack any practical sense of fight or flight. Often, I wonder if I can even take myself seriously."

"You are at a crossroad, Leonard," replied Monteocha. "All prophets and ascended masters transcend their vocabulary. They live in an eternal presence. You have been living out of your past history and bad habits, playing the same broken record over and over again. You get high on being low and by reliving familiar memories that loop back on themselves. Your brain doesn't know the difference between a real live experience and an imagined one. You stay in the cloud fishing out dead memories that take you to the end of your tether. You've reached an event horizon, where you realize how little control you have over the external world. What you call the 'end of your vocabulary' is a confrontation with the mercurial nature of consciousness. You're beginning to resist having your consciousness hijacked by the fixations of what most consider to be the ordinary world. Once you realize that 'no one steps in the same river twice,' and face this principle, the more you will be able to deconstruct years of negative programming and future hardships. In facing this universal human condition, things stop happening to you, but for you. Ironically, your end could be your beginning."

"I do not know, nor am I convinced, that there is a life after death. I think about taking my life, but am afraid to do so. Why? It comes down to the fear of death and what may come. The experience of fear keeps my vocabulary, the grand total of my mental life and acts, in check. I guess that I am fortunate that, even if I do not take myself seriously, I take fear seriously, yet do not know exactly where to turn. I would hope to cross the boundary of my insecurities into a worthwhile and meaningful future."

"To say that you have reached the end of your vocabulary is a first step in knowing yourself. You believe that your mind is your brain. Well, it's not. Your brain is a sense organ. Your mind is currently a web of personal biases that lead to nowhere, what you call the end of your vocabulary. Your journey begins by clearing your mind. The universe has heard your call. Take a vacation to the West Coast, Leonard; go to Mt. Shasta, California. There will be others to help guide you into the love that transcends a timeworn vocabulary to a restored narrative."

Leonard watched Monteocha disappear in front of his eyes. He then experienced himself being lifted up and floated back into the camper and came to rest on his bed. He opened his eyes and listened to the night noises. Finally, he went to sleep.

CHAPTER 2

REUNION

Did Leonard immediately dash out to the West Coast? No, he motored to Franklin, Tennessee, where he hooked up with Jeff Reynolds. He grew up with Jeff. They were both what you might describe as 'outdoorsy'. Both did just enough to get by in school and spent most of their time hunting, camping, fishing, and playing football. They both played football at Middle Tennessee State University, a stone's throw down the road. Jeff was the 'big guy' weighing 250 pounds playing nose guard. Leonard was a wide receiver at 175 pounds. During their junior year at the University, Leonard tore his ACL in the first game of the season. He dropped football, and became more interested in his studies. On the practical side, he focused on computer programming; on the not-so-practical side, he doubled up on his studies in philosophy.

When Leonard reached his hometown, he gave Jeff a call, and they agreed to meet at Starbucks on the Square. After taking a seat, Jeff looked over at Leonard with a surprised expression and remarked, "Boy, Leonard, you have changed. I remember when you'd never pay $2.00 for a small cup of coffee. You swore never to step foot in a Starbucks!"

Leonard grinned and shook his head. "Call it a knee jerk reaction – the first thing that came to mind. It doesn't matter what the cost. I'm rich."

"Oh, you're what?"

"Yeah, I made a lot of money."

"And how did you do that?"

"By changing my approach to day trading. I did that by using social media to buy a shit stock. The crowd wants a free ride, even free trades, and free profits. That illusion can move markets. Have you ever heard of GameStop?"

"Yeah, it went through the roof recently when hedge fund managers got caught in a short squeeze."

"Well, I played my part by writing a trading program for the crowd to download for free. It gave buy and sell signals on GameStop, and these signals appeared to work in real time. Thinking that social media would move the stock, a number of hedge fund managers jumped in with the crowd. Most of them had already shorted the stock on the way up. Those with short positions couldn't all get out at the same time, so I traded the stock as it took off. I got out just in time. After that, it wasn't long before trading houses halted any buying." Leonard paused and took on a serious look. "Jeff," he said, "I became addicted, not only to trading, but to social media; being possessed is not good. I don't want to be a part of that crowd. I want to get back to the outdoors, maybe do some fishing and hunting. On the return from Florida, I couldn't stop thinking that I needed to go back home."

"Well come on home, pal!"

"Jeff, did you tell me you took over your father's real estate business?"

"I guess that you could say that. Dad hardly ever comes into the office these days."

"I want you to find me some rural property, some wooded area, with a pond. I'm out of here tomorrow morning, but I'll be in touch. You've got my phone number if you find something. Just text me if I'm unavailable."

"Why the rush? You can stay with us."

"I'd like to stay around, but I can't."

"Why not, Leonard?"

"There's something that happened to me that's not right. I seem to be at loose ends, and I need to share it with someone I can trust, and that's why I'm talking to you."

"I'm all ears, Leonard. We go back and there's nothing we didn't share with one another."

"I had this weird dream. The dream seemed very real, except when I shot this guy and he didn't die. It could have been in another time. I had a heart-to-heart talk with this strange man, a Seminole Indian. He disappeared in front of my eyes, and I floated back to my camper and opened my eyes. I remember him telling me to go out to California, to Mt. Shasta. Have you ever heard of the place?"

"Mt. Shasta? It doesn't ring a bell. It sounds like you need to get laid."

"Yeah, but maybe I need to be open to this dream and check it out."

"Just take care not to jump off the deep end. Leonard, follow your instincts and stay grounded."

"Jeff, that's what I needed to hear."

CHAPTER 3

ON THE ROAD AGAIN

It was in April when Leonard motored to Mt. Shasta, California. He was in no hurry to get there, making frequent stops along the way, like following road signs into curious places. One place was about an hour's drive across the Mississippi River into Arkansas. There, Leonard parked his camper in an out-of-the-way wilderness setting and settled in for the night. The next morning, just after sunrise, Leonard stepped out the camper to sip his coffee and engage the rustic setting. Shortly, he caught sight of a couple walking down the road toward him. One, a crusty looking old man, was carrying a pick axe. The other, a rather handsome looking middle-aged woman, was carrying a shovel. Both were carrying backpacks and wearing kakis and hiking boots. As they crossed paths with Leonard, the old man spoke up. "Don't see many folks in these parts. You found a nice place to camp."

"Yeah, there's a beauty in anything wild and untamed. Let me guess," said Leonard, glancing down at the pick axe and shovel. "You guys are archeologists." The two looked at each other, laughed, then turned back to Leonard. "We're prospectors," said the old man.

The woman added, "We're on a crystal dig. How about you; what are you up to?"

"I plan to hike around the area."

The old man pointed to an opening in the woods. "Just stay on that path; it will take you back around to this spot. You'll come out down that road, about a quarter mile. Don't veer off the path; this place is a wilderness from witch some have never returned."

Following the old man's direction, Leonard took the winding path that led him to a waterfall, a sinkhole, and a breathtaking panoramic view of the mountainous region. Late in the day, the path opened up onto the road leading to his camper. Walking into familiar territory, Leonard literally breathed a sigh of relief. Shortly after arriving back at the campsite, Leonard greeted the prospectors on their way out. "Did you guys find what you're looking for?" he asked.

"No, we didn't," replied the old man.

"We did find this," said the woman, handing Leonard a clear six-sided crystal, about four inches long.

Holding the stone in his hand, he noticed a rainbow of colors against his skin. "It's beautiful," he said. "That's enough to make my day."

"Then keep it," said the old man. "Put it in your pocket and carry it around; it will take you where you need to go."

"Thanks," said Leonard. "I need all the direction I can get."

"We're all looking for direction," said the woman.

Leonard turned to the old man and asked, "What were you guys looking for back there?"

"We're looking for the mother of all crystals," replied the old man.

"We're looking for the Arkansas Crystal," added the woman.

"That's interesting," said Leonard. "I've never heard of it. What's so special about the Arkansas Crystal?"

"Like I said," replied the old man, "the crystal that you hold in your hand will take you where you need to go. The Arkansas Crystal will take you beyond any local time or place."

"How would you recognize such a crystal?"

"You don't have to worry about recognizing it," said the old man. "It recognizes you, and it is drawn to you. You'll know it when you see it."

Leonard reached in his pocket and withdrew a sky-blue stone. He handed the stone to the woman. "I found this along a creek bed this afternoon. It may be a sapphire. Let this be my gift to you both. I hope that you find what you are looking for."

CHAPTER 4

Mount shasta

The day that Leonard arrived in Mt. Shasta he found himself at a 'new age' expo. The place was crowded with people who could have lived in the sixties. They dressed like hippies. When the crowd sampled the different booths, their sponsors all wore what appeared to be costumes. The Tarot card reader wore a gypsy outfit; the lady in white silk put Leonard under a pyramid to rejuvenate his energy. Her brochure showed other members of her community living in pyramids dressed in white silk. One fellow called himself Angel Feather and claimed to be a retired physicist. He talked like one, but dressed in buckskin and moccasins. One could not be sure that he was selling anything, but he was promoting acoustics, calling it 'music of the spheres.' Then, there was Lucy, sitting behind a table reading The *Portable Nietzsche*. Her attire seemed normal. When she looked up at Leonard over her reading glasses, he noticed her glowing brown eyes and short blond hair. Bending down he asked, "Do you read Nietzsche because you feel misunderstood or because you seek the position of an overcomer?"

She took off her glasses, stood up, looked Leonard directly in his eyes and smiled. "Hi, I'm Lucy Morgan; you're just the person I'm fated to meet."

"Hi," replied Leonard, introducing himself. "You look interesting behind those reading glasses; you read philosophy, and I hope that we are fated to meet."

"I'd like to answer your Nietzsche question, Leonard." replied Lucy, "I'll have to show you."

Leonard learned that Lucy taught an introductory philosophy course at the local community college and lived in town where she carried on a side business taking folks on guided tours. She handed him a business card and said that he should come the following day, and she'd show him around. She lived in a small house on Main Street next to a doughnut shop. He couldn't miss the place because she had a sign posted in her front yard.

Early the next day, Leonard walked onto the front porch and knocked on the door. When Lucy opened the door, he stepped into her story world, a world that he never expected. He walked in as she was toweling sweat from her brow. A large, short-haired dog named Herk (short for Hercules) and a cat named Baba sat quietly watching from the far corner of the room. Lucy pointed to the weight bench and dumb bells scattered around the living area and invited Leonard to join her. As they proceeded, Leonard could see down the front of her blouse that she had no tits to speak of, just a firm bulge of muscular cleavage. Muscles rippled over her entire body. She finished her workout with a lengthy set of push-ups, never bothered to shower, scrambled into a pair of jeans and put on a long sleeve shirt. She and Leonard walked out the back door to her jeep, and they were off on an all-day hike.

About mid-morning they came to a secluded waterfall and a nearby spring. Lucy stripped down and said it was time for a shower. She stepped under the waterfall and insisted that Leonard strip down and join her. He did, and shivered under the cold water of the falls.

When they moved out from under the falls, Lucy spoke up, finally answering Leonard's Nietzsche question. "When I stand under the cold water, I don't feel misunderstood, rather, I feel like I'm one with the moment and that my head is clear. It's a way of overcoming my natural limits."

"I'm not sure I want to overcome these limits," said Leonard shivering.

"It takes practice to adapt to the experience," said Lucy. "Are you ready to do it again?"

"Lucy, you're kidding."

"Don't you want to overcome your own limits? Live dangerously, Leonard."

Lucy took Leonard by the hand and hurried him to a nearby spring. According to her, they were ready to rinse off. She jumped in and pulled him in with her. When they surfaced, she was bubbling with laughter. Leonard was expecting the shock of cold, but expressed surprise when he found it to be a warm spring.

There was something very childlike about Lucy. Everything she touched or saw was magnified in her eyes. There was no animal or plant that she wasn't amazed by. When they arrived back at her place and stepped out of the jeep, she greeted Herk and Baba with baby talk, and they showered her with affection in return.

That evening they dined at her place. She scampered about the kitchen preparing trout, salad, and homemade bread. She savored her food and delighted in the taste of a vintage wine. Her energy was boundless. She assured Leonard that they had only explored the landscape of Mt. Shasta and now needed to meet some of her friends. She invited Leonard to keep his camper in the parking lot behind her house, and they'd continue the tour the next day.

CHAPTER 5

LEONARD MEETS JAY

Leonard met Jay the next afternoon. He drove in from LA to spend a few days with Lucy. Jay looked to be in his early twenties: tall, lean, lots of red hair and a neatly trimmed beard and mustache. Although she didn't look it, Lucy was ten years his senior. Their relationship seemed to be something like a big sister/little brother connection. Lucy was a perplexing woman. She had two quite noticeable sides of her personality, an ethereal side which manifested itself in abstract, philosophical reflection, and an earthy side, which was the dominant side. Lucy was grounded -- outdoorsy and sensual, in touch with her pets and friends, a caretaker of sorts. Jay, on the other hand, seemed ungrounded: he lived in his head, or in some other world. Leonard noticed this the first time they met.

Lucy and Leonard were in her living room waiting for Jay's arrival, and, when Jay arrived, Leonard opened the front door and invited him in. Lucy walked over and introduced Leonard as Mr. Leonard Peters, a seeker. Leonard extended his hand, and Jay took hold of it with a firm grip.

Jay remarked, "Seeker, Mt. Shasta draws seekers."

Leonard's spontaneous reply was, "Have you found what you've been looking for?"

Jay stared into Leonard's face as if somehow Leonard had caught him off guard. He turned away, closed his eyes, and went into a kind of reverie. He began to mumble, then turned to Leonard with eyes wide open and replied. "Yes, Mr. Peters, I have found what I've been looking for. It's all around you, right in front of your nose. Then he turned the question around: "Have you found what you've been looking for, Leonard?"

"Jay, I can't say that I have."

Lucy broke into the conversation. "Air is what's all around, right in front of our noses, Jay."

Without retreating back into his reverie, Jay turned to Lucy, and calmly replied: "Air is not a subtle body." He leaned over and blew a puff of air onto Lucy's forehead. "Information is not like air. Air fuels the body; information fuels the mind. Air and information work together and form a living bridge to the new you."

"A library or the World Wide Web is filled with information," said Leonard. "There's nothing subtle about that."

"That's true, Leonard, but card catalogues are a thing of the past and so are physical libraries. We now tune into information. Most people do this with a smart phone or computer. I tune in with my mind."

"And, how do you do that, Jay?" asked Leonard.

"I clear my mind."

"What about taking on the mind of Christ?" asked Lucy.

"That's getting the cart before the horse, Lucy. The parable of the Sower and the Seed tells of man who scatters the Word of God all around. That seed doesn't all land on fertile ground. A mind has to be ready to receive the Word. That mind has to be clear, not full of chatter and cob webs.

The Word takes root in a person's body; it's a lived experience. The Incarnation is not merely ideational."

Addressing Jay, Leonard asked, "Are you saying that we have to clear our minds of unreliable mental baggage?"

"Something like that, Leonard. I think that your mind is taking a turn. Whatever you might think about your personal direction, you're not confronted with a dead-end. What you and Lucy both have reached is the end of chatter. You both are ready to take a leap into the quantum universe. Getting a real glimpse of more than you ever imagined will take you to a whole new level of motivation. Your aim, if you so choose, could be to take on the mind and body of Christ."

CHAPTER 6

THE TRIP TO OREGON

Lucy planned for the group to visit Lawrence, also referred to as Merlin, who lived in Ashland, Oregon. On the way, a conversation began in the front seat of the car. Jay looked over at Leonard and asked, "Do you think it odd that I mumble and go in and out of a trance?"

"Yes, it is rather odd. Isn't that what crazy people do? They find thoughts being inserted into their heads."

"So, you think I'm crazy, maybe in need of medication?"

"I didn't say that, Jay."

"But you're thinking it, right?"

"How could you possibly know what I'm thinking?"

Jay retreated into his mumbling meditative state.

Leonard blew the horn, and Jay suddenly looked up.

Leonard asked: "Did you know that I was going to blow the horn?"

"No, I didn't, Leonard. Let me put it to you this way," said Jay, "We live in a world that deals out medication to folks who talk with spirits from the other side. It's not hard to predict what you might be thinking."

"I'll tell you what's been on my mind lately; I'll say it again: I've reached the end of my tether. I can't prejudge you or anyone else. I tell my friends that I've exhausted my vocabulary. The world that I experience bores me. I don't feel the need to sell you on anything, including medication. Maybe, I need to reimagine my world because the world that I'm living in just doesn't quite connect. I can only guess into the future, based on what's happening now. Donald Trump, with a vocabulary of lies, cliches and platitudes will convince a confederacy of idiots into believing that the upcoming election could be rigged. It's a set-up for folks to believe a lie. Trump's not going to accept a loss, even without evidence to support that claim. There will be no smooth transition of power in the upcoming election."

Bowing his head, Jay slipped back into his trance mode. After a moment of silence, he began to mumble, as if carrying on a conversation in his head. Finally, he looked up and remarked, "They are making book on what you just predicted."

"Did I hear you correctly? You're saying that these 'entities' are making book on a smooth transition of power in the next presidential election?"

"Yes, if Trump loses, he's not going to relinquish his power. They are betting that the Civil War will be brought forward."

"That's crazy!" exclaimed Leonard.

"It is crazy, but that's what these 'little people' do; it's like a game. The enjoyment is about the power of prediction. You could say that they are sharpening their psychic abilities."

"I'm sick of video games. These little bastards that you're referring to are no different than we are, and the structure of their reality can't reach into anything more than a fantasy. It's surreal, betting on whether people in high places will deny the outcome of the upcoming election without any evidence to back up the claim."

"Patterns, my friend," said Jay, "patterns of fools and cult leaders put out a sound that registers with those who live

19

in fear and desperation. It's not unreasonable for a throng to undermine democracy by way of lies."

"That's not like the American people," remarked Leonard.

"I wouldn't bet on it," said Jay, then he slipped back into his own world. A few seconds passed before Jay looked up and changed the subject.

"The fifth vehicle that will pass going the other way will be a green Chevy. You will pass a car and the next car will have a license plate that reads: 'I see you'."

They waited several minutes. One, two, three and four vehicles passed. The fifth car to fly by was a green Chevy. Leonard drove around the car in front of him, and the car had a license plate that read: "I see you."

Jay smiled. "See what I mean – they're watching."

"Someone or something might be watching, but I can't say that I'm impressed. A ghost could be fucking with your brain, Jay. I mean, we're traveling on a one-dimensional highway. Set a camera in a drone, and you could go out in time and see what's headed your way."

"And that's what we do in life," said Jay, "It's all about predicting the future, even shaping the future. Not only do these entities give me guidance, I can remote view the upcoming traffic. These beings are multidimensional; some are present to get our attention, to help us; others are about making mischief."

"You mean something like a guardian angel?"

"Yeah, and you have encountered a guardian angel. You see, I've been expecting your visit to Mt. Shasta. The spirit guide, Monteocha, informed me of your coming."

"I didn't tell you that."

"You didn't have to, and you didn't have to tell me that you made a killing in the stock market. And, by the way, don't think that you were entirely responsible for that good fortune."

"Damn!" exclaimed, Leonard. "You're right, and I thought I had a vivid dream on the Monteocha Road. Now, I'm wondering if it isn't all one big dream."

"It is a big dream, and I'm available to help you. The fact is that you need training wheels."

Leonard took on a quizzical expression and turned to Jay, "Training wheels?"

"Yeah, but you'll have to trust me on that. You can't understand or travel to other dimensions without being grounded in this one. The sum total of your vocabulary is totally anchored to this world. That's why your 'ship won't sail'."

"What and where are these training wheels?" asked Leonard.

"These training wheels have a specific location in time and space; they are made from matter. The mansion world of heaven has no certain dwelling place; it is endless and timeless in the heavens. In your time, the location of this object will come into your experience. You will recognize it, and you will remember this day and what I have told you."

There was a note of sarcasm in Leonard's voice. "So, it's now a big mystery?" Leonard glanced over at Jay with a smirk. "Fortunately, I don't have to program more video games."

"That's true, but that's not your problem. I do some of the same work that you do, Leonard. Aside from writing animation programs for Disney, I remote view the future and pull up novel plots that will sell. Unlike you, I'm not bored by any of it."

Leonard gave no response.

"It's no use trying to figure it out, Leonard," said Jay, "So, stop trying. You can't fit into your own training wheels; training wheels are outside of your control. It's like trying to pull yourself up by your own bootstraps. Just enjoy having a vacation. Try to appreciate what comes to you."

"It sounds like you are asking me to give my power over to training wheels."

"You have no power, Leonard. When you come into your power, you'll gladly give up all props. Keep an open mind."

CHAPTER 7

ANGEL FEATHER SHOWS HIS MAGIC

The morning before the trip to Oregon, Lucy took Leonard to visit Angel Feather. On the way, Lucy looked over at Leonard and asked, "When we first met, do you remember me saying, 'You're just the person I'm fated to meet'?"

Leonard perked up and turned to her. "Of course, I do."

"Do you desire me?"

"What do you think?"

"How would you like to take a physical passion to a whole new level, Leonard?"

"I'm not sure what you mean by 'a whole new level'."

"That's because you can't imagine a healing experience beyond physical passion." Lucy took on a seductive expression. "We're about to find out if we resonate on the same frequency."

They drove a short distance outside of town and turned down a secluded dirt road which led to a solitary yurt among surrounding pines. The brook nearby revealed a turbine in the midst of a small waterfall.

Angel, a tall slender fellow, looked the same as he did at the expo, wearing his buckskin outfit and moccasins. He greeted the two on the porch of the circular structure and invited them in.

Upon entering, Leonard found himself in the presence of a white light, a contrast to the early morning light outside. Leonard blinked his eyes, as if to adjust to the surroundings. "This is amazing," he said, as he looked around. It was clear that the yurt sat on a flat rock. In the center of the room was a square box sitting on the natural stone floor. Mounted on the box was a thin circular stone table top. About a third of the interior space was devoted to amenities: a place to cook, shower, and sleep. The other two-thirds comprised a work space with an assortment of electronic equipment. There were no windows, giving the walls an odd look. Angel pointed out that the walls were composed of a material designed to fluctuate to the Schumann resonance. Leonard looked up at a pointed ceiling where spokes converged forming a hub directly above the stone table top.

Angel led the couple into the work area. Leonard took note of a collection of musical instruments: Native American drums, a flute, several chimes, a digeridoo, and a number of stringed instruments. A series of pictures or graphs hanging on the wall caught Leonard's eyes, and he walked over to get a closer look. In the center of the collection hung a depiction of Salvadore Dali's *Christus Hypercubus*.

Leonard turned to his host and Lucy, as if pleasantly surprised. "That's one of my favorite paintings. I saw it in the Metropolitan Museum of Art several summers ago while passing through New York City. Christ is being crucified on a tesseract, an unraveled hypercube. It expresses what we can't grasp."

"I agree," said Angel. He then pointed to the framed depictions on either side of the hypercube. "The pictures are merely two-dimensional figures, made up of simple circles -- mandalas. They are graphs of sounds, moving from low to high frequency. This place is all about frequency. The earth's electromagnetic frequency resonates around 7.83 hertz. We are all in tune with it. The fluctuation of this frequency affects our consciousness and ultimately our well-being."

Angel, noticing Leonard's calloused finger tips, took up a classical guitar from its stand and handed it to Leonard. "Here – take it -- play something for us."

Leonard hesitated. "I don't play in front of others."

"How you play doesn't make any difference," insisted Angel. "Take the guitar, Leonard."

Leonard strapped on the guitar, looked at Lucy, and winked. "This is for you, Lucy." Standing, he played through Francisco Tárrega's *Adelita*.

Having finished the piece, he turned to Angel with a look of amazement. "That's the most incredible sound system I've ever heard. What's this room hooked up to?"

Lucy moseyed over by Leonard. "That was nice, Leonard. Thank you." Smiling, she looked up into his eyes. "This room isn't hooked up to anything; it has natural acoustic properties."

"Let me show you what she's talking about," said Angel. Moving to the center of the room, he picked up a bucket of white powder and began to dust the stone table top. When he'd completed the task, he took up the digeridoo and blew into it. A deep tone filled the room and reverberated with the sound of *aum*. Leonard watched in amazement as the powder on the table transitioned into concentric rings. As Angel changed the pitch, the patterns changed. These were the two-dimensional patterns that had been photographed and hung on either side of the *Christus Hypercubus*.

25

Angel went on to explain. "It's not just the architecture of the room that affects sound. In fact, the yurt structure has less to do with the vibrations than the natural environment. Let me show you what I mean." Using his foot, Angel pushed a petal on the box under the table top which lowered wheels at all four corners, then rolled the table top and box aside. Clearly visible was a crystal-clear spring boiling within the surrounding rock. Leonard shook his head in disbelief.

"It's not exactly what you'd call magic, maybe a bit mystical," remarked Angel. "The box acts as a transducer. The surface of the table top is in sync with the box and arranges the dust particles in frequency patterns. Water coming from a spring circulates through any number of openings in this rock. That's why this well doesn't overflow; thousands of gallons flow through this spot every hour. The rocks, themselves, catch the flow -- they hum. You could say that the rock, on which this yurt rests, can sing."

"You act and think like a scientist," remarked Leonard. "How in the world did you get dubbed 'Angel Feather'?"

"I got named that at MIT and somehow it caught on here when my friends came around to check out what I was up to. In the lab, I set up an acoustic experiment in levitation using a feather. My associates insisted that I wasn't using an ordinary feather. They accused me of using an 'angel feather' and that wouldn't count. Leonard, you saw configurations merge out of a two-dimensional flat surface. When the method brought acoustics into a three-dimensional spatial framework, the sound lifted a feather right off a flat surface. Sound can lift more than one can imagine; now I'm levitating ping pong balls. The denizens of Mr. Shasta 'get off' on names that ignite mystery; I dress up like an indigenous person and play right along." Angel paused and chuckled. "In this room soul mates connect on the same Schumann Resonance, but it hasn't worked for me or Lucy."

VALIS

"Shame on you, Angel," joked Lucy. "You don't know what I need."

"I agree," said Angel, "You simply can't manipulate a soul. The soul is lighter than an angel's feather." Angel paused and fetched the classical guitar. "Here, Lucy, take it and play Leonard a piece."

Lucy took the guitar, turned to Leonard and winked. "This is for you, Leonard, enjoy." Lucy sat down on a wooden chair and assumed the formal position of a virtuoso classical guitarist. Flawlessly, she played through Tárrega's *Capricho Árabe*. When she finished, she wiped a tear from her cheek.

Leonard walked over to Lucy. "That was breathtaking. Your soul isn't linked to anything but beauty."

The following afternoon, Leonard woke up in Lucy's bed. Her bare arm was draped across his chest; he could feel her naked leg wrapped over his thigh. Her smell, her taste, her touch seemed like a familiar memory, something like a past experience, that he'd eventually wake up to and know that they were fated to meet.

27

CHAPTER 8

THE VISIT

Lawrence's place was located on several acres just outside Ashland, Oregon. The group included Angel, Lucy, Leonard, and Jay. Lawrence took the opportunity to show his guests around. His house and grounds came right out of medieval England as in the *Lord of The Rings*. There were stones and crystals scattered about, flowing streams, green ferns, hanging baskets, a koi pond, and a mini hobbit house for guests. There was a wooden sign above the threshold of Lawrence's front door which read "Merlin's Place."

There was an upstairs and a basement; Lawrence lived in the basement. The upstairs consisted of two rooms, one room for meditation and music, and the other a healing area. The upper living space was not in the least cluttered; a single painting hung over a couch revealing a mandala with a 'flower of life' in the center. Stained glass windows produced a blue tone that permeated the room.

The work area was used as a place of healing. The centerpiece was a wooden table used for energy work, covered with what looked to be lamb's wool. There were colored lights penetrating a crystal skull. Mirrors hung around the room. There were singing bowls, side tables filled with crystals and colorful rocks, as well as pictures of persons Lawrence referred to as 'ascended masters,' including Merlin and Jesus. An assortment of digeridoos and Native American flutes were positioned by one of the side tables. Fashioned in the form of triangles, copper tubing hung from the ceiling over the table and encased a cowhide drum. It was dazzling and overpowering. Movement and color were everywhere, creating an expectation of strange sounds.

Just before the return to Mt. Shasta, Lawrence and Angel went into the work area. Lawrence closed the door.

Jay sat on the floor in a lotus position, his palms up and his arms resting on his knees. His eyes were half-closed. Leonard and Lucy were sitting on the couch; Lucy leaned over and whispered in Leonard's ear, "He's remote viewing Lawrence and Angel."

Jay laughed, "I am not remote viewing. I couldn't anyway because you guys keep talking. Be quiet so I can tune into the other two."

Lucy sat up in her seat, "Jay, you have no business meddling in their conversation."

"It's funny," replied Jay, "They're trying to bring coherence into that room. Lawrence wants to rearrange the room in order to levitate his patrons." Jay stops and listens, then goes on. "Angel says it's possible to levitate someone through sound, but not likely. Sound waves push up, but the pull of gravity is stronger than the push from sound. Angel says he's tried all sorts of 'bells and whistles' to increase the push but couldn't lift more than a ping pong ball."

Lucy stood up and stopped the flow of words. "I don't want to hear anymore, Jay, I want to go."

CHAPTER 9

THE BLACK CROW

On the return to Mt. Shasta, Jay retreated into one of his meditative states. After a short while, he opened his eyes and spoke. "There's a Buddhist monastery up ahead. A bird is calling me."

Leonard turned off the highway and headed in the direction of the monastery. A gate prevented them from entering the monastery grounds. On a nearby hill, they observed a path leading to a colorful pavilion. Pointing to the pavilion, Jay proclaimed again, "A bird is calling me from that path."

The group could not make out the contents of the shelter until they arrived. The opening of a framed structure had an upper and lower part; the upper part contained an enclosed figure of the Buddha and the lower part contained several rows of revolving prayer wheels. The interior of the structure was painted with Buddhist symbols from the ancient Tibetan tradition.

Jay found what he was looking for just outside the pavilion; on the ground was a rather large black crow. Clearly, the bird was dead; rigor mortis had set in. Leonard and Lucy watched as Jay bent down over the bird and went in and out of his usual reverie. Jay looked up and said, "It's not dead yet." His posture and tone were reverent and respectful. "The spirit of the bird is crossing over; it's not there yet, but will be shortly. It's telling me that my time is short."

On the way to the car, Lucy pleaded with Jay not to be so morbid. She tried to convince him not to fixate on death. Lucy assured Jay that he didn't need to 'check out' because he had much to offer his friends and family.

"Friends and family, you say," replied Jay. "That's the very reason I am called to 'check out,' Lucy!"

Angel heard the comment and let the subject of death alone, rolled his eyes and appeared totally at a loss for words.

When they got back in the car, heading back to Mt. Shasta, Jay turned to Leonard and said, "It's one thing to read about Buddhism, omens, death and dying, but it's quite another to meet the unknown. I'm not facing the unknown; I've lived many lives and am able to access all of them. Lucy treats me like a little brother. She wants to protect me from death. For her, death is a big problem."

Jay paused as if to gather his thoughts. "Let me be straight with you. The next time we meet, I'll be transformed, and you'll be fully open to the dharma or teaching. Your training wheels will be in your possession. You and Lucy can take a spin on them. After that, you won't need me; hopefully you'll be enlightened and on your own."

"Prayer wheels, training wheels, who are you, Jay?"

"I'm an old soul in what looks to you like a young body," said Jay. "I learned to die many lifetimes ago. It's no biggie. You haven't yet learned to die. Your own tradition – Christianity -- teaches about dying and being born again."

"Yeah," replied Leonard, speechless. "I believe that being born again is a matter of being transformed, changed into a loving person."

"It's not just about being a nice guy, Leonard. You have to take it to another level."

"What exactly do you mean, 'take it to another level'?"

"The good book says that what's bound in this world is bound in the next. You don't believe in what you can't see. You can't see these other worlds because you live on a purely survival level, which are the three energy centers (chakras) below your heart. You've got to ascend the heart and go above to get a bird's eye view. Once you get that view, and it makes a deep enough impression, you'll be off the training wheels. Yes, Leonard, death, crossing over, whatever you want to call it, will not cause you to be overcome by fear and flight. You will not be compelled to compromise higher principles."

"Well, tell me how I can get a peek, even thru a crack."

"The first thing is learning to be quiet; your mind is too noisy. You need to learn to be quiet and listen. That's mostly what it means to pray."

"I pray every day."

Jay declared, "No, you don't! You don't even know how to listen or what to ask for. You're are at the end of your vocabulary and fear death."

"How do you know that, Jay?"

"Don't take yourself so seriously, Leonard. I've read your mind, know your thoughts, and you resist what your senses can't detect. I'm transitioning out of here to help you and Lucy develop mature souls."

"What!" exclaimed Leonard.

"You need to chill out, Leonard, and be still. You're so hyped up on adrenalin that you can't think straight. There is nowhere to run. Did it ever occur to you that help is on the way?"

"So, you're going to set me up with training wheels. That sounds bazar."

"Leonard, just chill out. You're not in the driver's seat, not yet. You're a passenger; just keep your eye on the road." Jay hesitated and quipped, "And, by the way, don't forget to use your rear-view mirror."

CHAPTER 10

MEETING AT THE LAVA TUBE

While Lucy went to teach a class, Leonard proceeded to visit a lava tube just outside of town. He walked over a desert-like terrain until he came to the huge opening of what looked to be a cave. He walked in and saw that it resembled a tunnel with an opening at the far end, about 100 yards away. Shortly, he saw a man appear at the far end, motioning Leonard to approach him. When Leonard reached him, the man looked familiar, but Leonard couldn't remember his name or where he had seen him.

"Haven't we met?" asked Leonard.

"Yes, we have."

"Please, remind me."

"I'm Monteocha, the man you met in Florida, with a more modern appearance."

"Yeah, the one I saw in a dream. Surely, I'm not dreaming, now."

"No, not really, but you are in a conscious state that will allow you to remember. You do want to deal with your issue?"

"My issue?"

"A man who has exhausted his vocabulary has to recover his memory. You think that your memories are in your head, but they aren't; memories are stored in the Akashic cloud, a vast living intelligent network; your brain is merely a sense organ. Come, follow me and I'll show you what I'm talking about."

After walking to the center of the tunnel, Monteocha directed Leonard's attention to the wall of the cave. "There are some things that you need to carry forward," said Monteocha. "What you are about to see will be directed to your heart, not your intellect. You will see and desire by way of your emotions. Eventually, you will wake up out of your slumber and have no problem remembering."

Leonard looked up at the wall and saw a movie playing; he was not just viewing the movie. He was in it. He saw himself in his camper answering a text from his friend, Jeff. The text read: "Come home, I've located rural property that meets your needs. I have a 30-day purchase agreement; if you don't buy it, I will." Next, the scene switched to Leonard and Lucy making love the previous evening.

When the scene ended, Leonard turned to Monteocha and remarked, "I don't remember a text message from Jeff."

"That's true, but you will remember the text when you leave here. Just look on your phone; you'll find it." Monteocha looked into Leonard's eyes and addressed him in a more serious tone. "Leonard, how do you feel about Lucy?"

"I've never felt this way about any other woman. She's talented and beautiful. I don't see her wanting to be with me. Why would she give a shit about someone like me?"

"Why not? If you forget what she said and how she gave herself to you, she might just let you slip away. Before you return home, remind her that she was right, that 'you're just the person she was fated to meet'."

The final movie on the cave wall was much longer. It was in black and white, with a date indicating that the time period of the presentation was November 30, 1864.

From a rural farmhouse on the outskirts of Chapel Hill, Tennessee, the sound of cannon fire could be heard in the area around Franklin, fifteen miles away. Dawn had broken when a small band of Confederate soldiers rode up and dismounted in front of a log cabin.

General Forrest ordered his men to water the horses and glanced over at a nearby well. He hurriedly walked onto the porch, knocked on the door and shouted, "Tom, Tom, open the door!"

A dirty tattered and torn young woman opened the door. Her blind eyes were fixed and filled with tears. The blind girl stood back as Forrest walked in leaving the door open. At the far end of the room, stretched out on the floor was a large cigar-shaped crystal, approximately five foot long. General Forrest stopped, winced, and cried out, "Oh my God, no!" Forrest slowly walked to a wooden bench in front of the crystal. He looked over at the blood-soaked body spread out on it.

Weeping, the blind girl spoke up. "They killed him with a sword, Mr. Forrest, just up and struck him down."

"My brother was a fine young man," said Forrest. "Many more good men will die today." Forrest stepped back and looked the girl over. "You're pregnant, nigger." The girl stood silent. "I could kill you, but I think not. You've not failed me; you've always been right." General Forest paused. "You're free, on your own now."

Forrest moved out onto the porch where he confronted a nervous lieutenant. The blind girl followed him.

"General Forrest, sir," said the lieutenant, "there's nothing left here: grain, powder, or livestock. Nothing, sir. It's all gone."

Forrest gave the lieutenant a stern look. "There's a large crystal inside. You boys, muscle it out and pitch it in the well." Forrest hesitated, as several of his men reacted to the command. "Wait," he said. "They killed the sergeant, and we don't have time to carry a dead man. Pitch him in the well."

As the troop galloped away, the blind girl made her way to the well. Standing over the opening, she spoke out: "You will rise again."

When the screen went blank, Monteocha asked, "What do you recall about that?"

"Nothing," said Leonard.

"What did you feel, Leonard?"

"A Civil War was going on. I felt resentment for racial bigotry and stupidity. It looked like an interesting piece of history. I wanted to see more."

"You have to remember, and then you can carry it forward, Leonard."

"I don't understand."

"You will. Keep your eye on the rear-view mirror."

CHAPTER 11

LEONARD REUNITES WITH JEFF

Leonard pulled his worn pickup truck into a vacant parking lot of a rural volunteer fire department with camper in toe. It was a bright day and pleasantly warm. Stepping out of the truck, he gazed across the street at a winding creek that bordered a freshly plowed field. Leonard took a deep breath, taking in the smell of fresh dirt. It was 2021 and time for a new life.

Leonard quickly removed a sweatshirt, tossed it through the window of the cab, and then moved to the front of the truck where he used the front fender to facilitate a stretching routine. Minutes later, he looked down at his wristwatch and walked out to the road where he saw a Cherokee Jeep racing toward him.

The jeep pulled into the parking lot. Jeff rolled down the window and greeted Leonard with a smile. Jeff parked beside Leonard's camper and jumped out. The two men laughed and gave each other several elbow bumps, as the COVID-19 was in full force.

"How does it feel to be back from your vacation?" asked Jeff. "I take it that you're ready to settle down."

"It feels right. And I am ready to settle down, at least, for a while. So, let's go look at the property you've found."

"There's something odd going on," said Jeff. "I get a text from you, and you're wanting to hook-up at the Flat Creek Community Center."

"How so?" replied Leonard.

"That's near where I found your property."

"Yeah, right. You texted me about procuring it last week."

"Leonard, I didn't find the property until yesterday."

"What?" questioned Leonard, pulling out his phone and bringing up his text messages. "You sent a message a week ago saying you'd found the property." Leonard, looking at the messages, said, "Jeff, it's not there; your text is not there."

Jeff looked into the messages and remarked, "No, it's not, but there's your message to me: 'I'll be home next Thursday; let's hook-up at Flat Creek. More later'."

"This doesn't make sense, Jeff. I knew about the property before you found it. Is this property about 2 miles from here?"

"Probably less than that."

"Well, I'm not going to bog down in contradictions. Let's jog on over and take a look."

The short run gave the two men a chance to do some catching up. "I'm glad your marriage to Betty has lasted; I would have never guessed it."

"Yeah," I know," replied Jeff. "That's why you dumped her off on me."

"I what?"

"Yeah, I remember, back in the dorm you were saying that she was not your type, and you invited me to 'try her out'."

The two men laughed and Leonard remarked. "Twelve years is a long time. Does she look the same?"

"She works out and looks great." Jeff paused and pointed to a side road. They made a left turn and were making their way toward a fenced pasture up ahead. When they came to the fence, Jeff turned to Leonard and asked, "Last time we met you said that you made a bundle in the market. Why are you still driving around in an old beat-up pickup and a trailer that's seen its day?"

"The first thing on my shopping list is rural property. I'll keep the old Ford, and settle for a brand-new Airstream. The last thing on my list is a vintage *Indian Chief* motorcycle, with a side-car, like Uncle Hoover's."

"Yeah, Leonard, I'll never forget those bolts around the block with your uncle. He was a really cool guy."

"Yes, I miss him. He was like a big brother. He didn't have a pot to piss in or a window to throw it out of, but he was good-natured. He'd give you the shirt off his back without a care in the world, and he was, somehow, situated in his game. I want to get there, Jeff, situated, and I'm not there yet. I feel like something is missing, and I'm not sure that it's something on a shopping list. Frankly, Jeff, I feel disoriented. Like the missing text message and knowing beforehand that you'd found this property."

"It's intuition or good instincts. Let's hop this fence and check out the first item on your list. We're almost there."

CHAPTER 12

THE RUIN

The two friends crossed over the fence and strolled to the far end of a field which led to a narrow path into the canopied woods of mostly shagbark hickory and white oak.

"This is the back way into the property," remarked Jeff. "This path comes out the other end, where we usually enter the place." About midway on the trail, Jeff stopped and looked around. "This is the place," he said, and he took Leonard into the opening of a cedar thicket.

Leonard's eyes opened wide, and he shook his head. "How in the hell did a log cabin get out here in this wilderness?"

"Things change over time. One hundred and fifty years ago the landscape must have been different. This land was probably cleared and farmed. This ruin opens us to the past."

"Wow!"

"Let's go check it out."

The two men stepped onto a rock, and then stepped down into the front opening and onto the dirt floor of a single room cabin about fifty by twenty. At both ends of the building there were piles of stone surrounding what must have been fireplaces. There were several openings in the log walls which once served as windows. The roof had long since fallen apart, and several pieces of tin were scattered about on the floor. A huge gnarled cedar tree grew up almost in the middle of the dwelling.

Leonard ambled to the back end of the cabin with his eyes fixed on the far wall and he touched it. Turning to Jeff, he said, "I can't believe this picture is still here; it's the only thing left in the cabin."

"What picture? I don't see any picture." When Leonard turned back to the wall, there was no picture. "My God, Jeff, I could have sworn that I saw a picture, a framed daguerreotype of a Confederate soldier and a woman."

"Weird stuff happens back here," explained Jeff. "I believe you. The first time I came into this place and looked out that window, I heard the sound of children at play, dogs barking, and roosters crowing. I went to the window, looked out all around and there was nothing, only the faint sound of children singing 'dig up and read, dig up and read.' There were no dogs or roosters or children at play. It gave me the willies."

"Really," said Leonard, as he looked in wonder around the interior of the ruin. "It's like I know this place, or I've been here before. Yet, I can't place it."

The two men went on their way and arrived at the front end of a wooded area which opened into a five-acre lot spotted with oak trees and shrubs. It was included in the property. In this opening there was a well house and beyond that a street. The street was the entrance to the property. At the back end of the lot was a concrete platform which appeared to be the beginning of an outbuilding.

Leonard pointed to the platform saying, "That foundation would be a good place to park my camper."

"Yes, it would be," replied Jeff, "a place to settle in." Jeff paused and went on. "I have a 30-day purchase agreement to buy this property. Old man Bradford, the Chapel Hill real estate agent, said that the owners had a doublewide trailer moved here from somewhere in the area. About a year later, they just up and left, and Bradford got a call to sell the place. He came to check it out and made an appraisal. He told me that whoever lived there left in a hurry: the beds weren't made, there were dishes on the table and rotting food was in the fridge. The property had been on the market long enough for Bradford to have it mowed. The sellers were asking $200,000 for the parcel. I offered them $100,000, thinking they'd meet me in the middle. Bradford called me back and agreed to my bid. This included a provision that the sellers could have the trailer towed away. Two days later the trailer was gone. I have no idea where they took it or if Bradford cut a deal and kept it for himself. It's weird how I came into this. Anyway, these 37 areas are yours if you want them. If not, I'm buying them."

"This is exactly what I've been looking for. I'm in."
"I'll set up the closing and give you a call, Leonard."
"Let's do it."

CHAPTER 13

THE CLOSING

The clerk looked up from a bundle of papers and said, "The title search is complete." She rose from her seat, stacked the pages, and hand delivered them to Leonard at the far end of the table.

Without reading the documents, Leonard signed the paperwork and handed the clerk a cashier's check.

"Well, that's it," said Jeff. "You're now the owner of your own personal property. Congratulations, my friend."

The two men walked out of the building onto the street, and took off their COVID masks.

"Where are you parked?" asked Jeff. "I don't see your truck; do you need a ride?"

"Thanks, but I'm parked across the street."

Jeff glanced across the street. He smiled, nodded, and looked over at Leonard. "Damn, you weren't kidding. You bought a motorcycle."

"Yep, that's a completely restored 1915 Indian Chief motorcycle with a side-car to boot."

"You must have paid a fortune for it!"

"Yep, more that I paid for the property." Leonard paused and smiled. "I appreciate the favor, old friend."

The two walked across the street, and Jeff stood there admiring the vintage bike.

"Get in and we'll take a spin around the block."

"Fire her up, Leonard, and let's ride!"

CHAPTER 14

Dig up and read

Within the week, Leonard had set up his new Airstream and an outbuilding on the cleared part of his property. Every day, sometimes two or three times a day, he explored the wooded area for a place to build. Late one morning he approached the secluded sanctuary of the old ruin. It was just before spring, right before the new growth could usher in a change in coloration. Upon arriving at the dilapidated structure, he walked in. The sunlight beamed through the window casting his shadow on the far wall. He heard what sounded like whispering sounds. He came to the window, looked out, and no one was there. There was no wind wafting across barren branches, only sunlight coming through the skeleton of trees. He heard the sound of children singing: "dig up and read. dig up and read." It was the same singing that Jeff reported earlier.

Looking for the source of the singing, Leonard stepped through the opening of an old window onto the ground. Though the sun was almost directly overhead, Leonard walked behind the cabin to a place where he noticed his shadow vanish. Looking up toward the blinding light of the sun, he again heard the whispering voices: "dig up and read. dig up and read."

Leonard turned his gaze to the ground, bent down on one knee, and began to sweep the debris away from what appeared to be a covering of sorts. Leonard removed a piece of metal roofing and saw what it had been covering a well, about thirty feet deep. The stones of the well had been carefully laid all the way down. The sunlight fell upon the bottom where the water appeared clear. A crystal aggregate, composed of many smaller crystals, could be seen emerging above the surface of the water. As the sun crossed over the opening, a rainbow of dots spiraled around the long narrow casing. As the sun passed, the colors vanished. The crystal formation, the water, the well walls: all looked like glimmering lights and shadows. As he left, Leonard heard the faint sound of the children singing: "dig up and read. dig up and read."

CHAPTER 15

Surprise

Leonard had just finished making coffee when he heard a knock on the door of his Airstream. He pulled the curtain to look out the window, then unlocked and opened the door.

"My God, Jeff, you look like hell. What happened?"

Jeff stood there not saying anything. He had a disheveled look that comes from having slept in his clothes. It could have been that sleep never came, only tossing and turning.

Leonard gave a nod for his friend to come in. Jeff stepped up into the Airstream and took a seat at the kitchen table and Leonard poured them both a cup of fresh coffee. He took a seat across from Jeff and asked, "So, what's going on?"

"I thought it strange," replied Jeff, "when Betty told me she wanted to get COVID behind us before having company over or gathering in a group. I didn't give it much thought until I remembered her not giving up the gym and questioned her about it. She told me that she was taking private lessons with a trainer since the gym was closed. She led me to believe that her trainer was a female. That was not the case. Apparently, her male trainer didn't bother to turn off the security camera. Someone, I don't know who, sent me a copy of their session."

"A video recording, of what?"

"When I watched the first segment, I had to turn it off."

"Does she know that you have the tape?"

"She knows."

"And?"

"She's gone, Leonard, living with her personal trainer. Maybe it's just a fling. Maybe she'll come to her senses."

Jeff covered his face with his hands and wept.

Leonard reached over and cupped his friend's hand. He could see the tears well up in Jeff's eyes. "Let it out, my friend, let it out."

CHAPTER 16

Dig it up

The weekend came and the weather had a touch of spring in the air. The day was clear; a calm breeze, and twenty-five percent of the American population had recently been vaccinated. Jeff drove up near Leonard's doorstep, beeped his horn, and watched as Leonard closed the door, walked toward his jeep and hopped in.

"Well, Jeff, how's it going?"

"Night sweats, man. Night sweats."

"I've got a solution for that: just drive over to the ruin. We're going to need your jeep today."

Jeff put the jeep in four-wheel drive and pulled onto the narrow road leading to their destination. Jeff wanted to know what the hell night sweats had to do with the ruin.

"Nothing at all! It's like this: we have the same problem; our problem is about control. You can't control that cheating bitch any more than I can control a life of sick habits. I've come home to reboot. There's nothing we can do, Jeff. Don't you see? It's about learning how to just be, like in the Beatle's song, *Let it Be*."

Jeff laughed and shook his head. "That sounds like pure bull shit, a cop-out. *Letting it be* sounds like letting go, and I'm not letting go of my wife; love doesn't burn out like a cigarette. I believe in second chances."

"Even if she comes back, you've got to let her go and take on a new mind, rewire, or whatever else you want to call it. Can you forgive that cheating cunt?"

Jeff brought the jeep to a stop and changed the subject. He looked to the opening leading to the ruin and asked, "Why don't we walk back there?"

"I'll show you why," said Leonard and motioned for Jeff to drive behind the ruin in order to show him the well he'd discovered. When they arrived, Jeff stopped the jeep, got out, and walked over to Leonard. Leonard bent over and removed the metal that covered the well. Jeff was surprised: "Sure is a well!" He kneeled and peered into it. Leonard took a flashlight from his pocket and lit up the bottom of the well. Turning to Jeff, he remarked, "Look at that."

"Give me the flashlight."

Jeff took the light and moved it in a circular motion around the bottom of the well. He saw the stone and a rainbow of colors twinkle as he rotated the light. "It looks like a crystal. That's the weirdest thing I've ever seen. How in the hell did it get down there?"

"I don't know but we're going to find out what's down there. Pull up the jeep, and we'll winch it out."

"Yeah, why not? Let's do it!"

After the two men cleared the brush, Jeff straddled the well with the two front wheels of the jeep. They made a loop in the winch cable and lowered it toward the target. The cable loop caught the crystal object and tightened. After several attempts to bring the object out of the mud, it broke loose and began to rise to the surface. Jeff backed up the jeep and pulled the crystal into full view. It was cigar-shaped, about five foot long.

"Leonard, this is amazing!"

"It's not just amazing; it's a coincidence, down right magical. Do you remember what you told me when you showed me this property? I heard the same thing that you did: 'dig up and read, dig up and read'. Now look what we've dug up."

After the two men pulled up the crystal, they placed it in the back of Jeff's jeep and drove back to the Airstream where they proceeded to transfer the crystal to Leonard's pickup and covered it with a tarp.

Before departing for Franklin, Jeff made the comment, "Now I've got something else to keep me awake."

"Think about it, Jeff. When have you ever been this alive?"

Jeff gave Leonard a hard look, smiled, and shook his head. "Be serious, Leonard."

Leonard laughed. "Thanks, my friend, thanks for your help. Come back and give your mind a rest."

"I'll think about it."

CHAPTER 17

THE CALL FROM LUCY

At the beginning of the following week, Leonard started buying tools and building materials. By the middle of the week, he got down to work. While clearing brush form the area, Leonard felt his phone vibrate, and cut off the chain saw to answer it. A spicy voice blurted out at the other end. "It's me, Lucy, your faithful Mt. Shasta tour guide."

"Goodness, Lucy. It's good to hear your perky voice! I've been meaning to call. Your energy always puts me in a good place. You've been missed, girl."

"Likewise, Mr. Wanderer."

"Not any more, Lucy. I've settled down in Tennessee."

"Oh! So, you're grounded."

"Yes, on 37 acres and ready to make what you call a vision quest."

"Well, excellent! I like to hear that!"

"You were right about opening up and going with the flow. Since then, things are falling in place. Things you would have to see to believe."

"That sounds like the new you, tuned up a couple of octaves. By the way, Angel Feather asked about you; he says that he's picking up on your vibes."

"I believe it. I'm trying out his advice."

"Cool."

"Remember the trip we took to Oregon?" I drove, Jay sat in the front seat, and you and Angel Feather sat in the back. Jay was fascinating, totally unique; I like him. Is he still in Shasta or did he return to LA?"

There was an extended silence on the other end. "Lucy, are you still there?"

"Yes, I'm here," Lucy paused, and let it out. "Jay killed himself one month ago today. It's sad. I tried to keep him in Shasta, but he left for LA to complete an animation project for Disney. I only know that he climbed a tower and was purported to have jumped off."

"God, I hate to hear it. He was so gifted; what a waste! Are you sure that it wasn't an accident? Maybe he just slipped and fell."

"No, he didn't slip and fall. He told you of his fate. He was suicidal; he went off the deep end, and I couldn't convince him otherwise or get him help."

"All of this sounds strange. I received a package in the mail today from Jay, a month late."

"Really?"

"Yes, really, a book by Phillip Dick, *VALIS*.

After a short silence, Lucy continued, "I had a dream last night. For some strange reason it prompted this call, and I'm not sure why. I saw Jay's face in the dream; three times he spoke. 'Pick up and leave...pick up and leave...pick up and leave.' Then I saw a motorcycle with a side-car; it looked like something from the past, but restored."

"Since last seeing you, Lucy, I bought a vintage Indian motorcycle with a side-car. You'll have to see what I've come across out here. I think I've stumbled into what Jay called training wheels. I want to see you. It's not like texting or talking on the phone. You keep me awake, and I need that.

Lucy, I miss you...   follow your dream: 'pick up and leave'...pack it all up and come to me."
"I will, Leonard."

CHAPTER 18

Symmetry

When Leonard heard Lucy's jeep, he hurried out of the Airstream to greet her. There she was, window rolled down, smiling, with Herk by her side and Baba ready to jump out the window. Lucy slowly opened the door, never taking her eyes off Leonard, and she gave him a hug. They walked hand and hand to the camper and stepped into it.

"Wow! This is sure a step-up from what you had."

Leonard smiled. "I thought you'd like it."

"I love it!"

"Plenty of room for the both of us." Moving toward the kitchen area, Leonard remarked, "I remember something about a special diet, and how you preferred distilled water with a twist of lime. What would you like?"

"The water will be fine."

Lucy sat down in a swivel chair, flipped off her loafers, and she looked around: "books, guitar, a good sound system, what more do you need?"

Leonard handed her the water with a lime twist. "What more do I need? I need you."

Lucy grinned. "You need me now. But what happens when you get bored with the books, the guitar, the sound system, and me? What happens when these things terminate your new vocabulary and the honeymoon is over?"

"Well, Lucy, we'll just have to sit back, at a distance, and play duets with classical guitars."

Leonard sat down in the swivel chair across from Lucy. He reached out with his bare foot and touched Lucy's big toe until his foot covered hers. She did the same.

"Symmetry is beautiful, Leonard. Two people, two feet, one foot up, one foot down with a twist of energy coming from both sides, male and female."

"Yes, it is – beautiful – and interesting."

"That's where Jay and I differed," said Lucy, "I'm old school. My mother was a devout Catholic. Her values run in my veins. I want to live in this world and affirm this world in all of its amazing symmetry. Actually, I want to be around for a while; I want to live and love, and experience being loved. Jay saw the world as a three-dimensional prison. Jay spoke of himself as an interdimensional time traveler; he read Phillip Dick and talked about a hidden order – not the imagined order of Phillip Dick, not A VAST ACTIVE LIVING INFORMATION SYSTEM, but A VAST ACTIVE LIVING INTELLIGENT SOUL. I don't want to think that Jay committed suicide."

"If Jay is right," replied Leonard, "and there are other worlds, maybe we have to live into and affirm this world before moving onto the next."

"The awesomeness of symmetry is in the transitions," replied Lucy, "the hurtful spaces in-between, when the feet grow old and calloused, and the strong connections get weak."

"There seems to be a symmetry in the occurrences that stretch from here to Mt. Shasta," said Leonard. "Jay knew of his transition. You saw Jay in a dream, and you're here. I received his package late – one month to the very day he died.

And there's more – a lot more. What happened in Mt. Shasta is unfolding right in front of our eyes – like an unusual coincidence. I'll have to show you what I'm talking about. We'll start with the Indian motorcycle, the one you saw in your dreams."

CHAPTER 19

DREAMS

Before dawn, Leonard opened his eyes and suddenly sat up, wide awake. He found Lucy's cat, Baba, on his haunches between his legs. "Oh, it's you, Baba. Is he hungry?"

Baba jumped down and Leonard threw his legs off the bed and stood up. He switched on the light. Looking down the hall toward the master bedroom, he saw the shadowy figure of Herk at the door looking back at him. Leonard closed the door to the hall so as not to wake Lucy and glanced down at Baba, purring and rubbing on his leg. Leonard opened a can of moist food, set it down, and proceeded to make himself a cup of coffee.

Lucy was up, put on a robe, and moved to the front of the camper. "Good morning."

"Well, good morning to you, Lucy. I hope you slept well."

"I did. I'm ready for the day."

Lucy looked down at Herk. He was wagging his tail and looking back at her. He barked and Lucy got up and opened the front door. Herk darted out and Baba followed. "They'll do their thing and explore the new territory."

"And that's what I'll show you today, the new territory. Coffee?"

"No thanks, just a bottle of warm water."

"Breakfast?"

"I eat just one meal a day."

"I didn't know that."

"Now you're getting to know my habits."

"You'd best wear long pants today. The woods are leafing out, and it may be a bit chilly this morning."

The two dressed for the occasion and stepped out into the early morning.

Before entering the woods, Leonard led Lucy to his motorcycle. He pulled back the tarp covering it. "Is this the restored Indian motorcycle you saw in your dream?"

"That's exactly what I saw in my dream."

"Wait to see what else I have to show you. Let's walk over to the truck."

Leonard opened the tailgate and threw back the tarp covering the huge crystal. "My friend, Jeff, helped me pull this gem out of a nearby well last week. Seeing is believing, Lucy."

"It's beautiful! I've seen a lot of crystals out my way; Lawrence is loaded down with them, but not one this size. It's amazing!"

"Early this morning," said Leonard, "I woke up out of a deep sleep. In a dream I saw a crystal like the one Jeff and I pulled out of the well. This crystal was polarized." Leonard withdrew a small pocket compass from his shirt pocket and directed it toward the crystal. He then moved around the truck and watched as the compass needle changed positions. Turning to Lucy, he handed her the compass. "Here, you try it." Lucy took the compass, looked into its face, and moved around the crystal. Leonard opened the tailgate of the truck and stepped back.

"Check it out from this side, Lucy."

60

Lucy moved behind the tailgate and pointed the compass toward the cigar-shaped stone; the compass pointed south, not north.

Lucy looked up and back down at the compass needle. "You're right, Leonard. The stone is drawing the needle in the wrong direction." The two looked at each other.

"Do you think that you can help me snake this thing out of the truck?" asked Leonard.

"Yes."

"Let's drive back to where Jeff and I found the crystal and pull it off the bed. I want to show you something."

"Sounds good, Leonard, let's ride."

CHAPTER 20

Skinny-Dipping: THE FOUNTAIN OF YOUTH

Leonard got down on his knees and removed the rusty tin covering over the well. Lucy bent over and peered in. Herk and Baba sat on their haunches nearby and watched.

Lucy turned to Leonard. "So, this is where you and Jeff found the crystal?"

"Yes, right down in the well. Why would folks dig a well, find a crystal, and leave it there?"

"I can't imagine," said Lucy as she stooped down beside Leonard.

Leonard took his flashlight and lit up the inside of the well. The two bent over and peered in.

"Is life like a well? You peer in and get darkness and mud." Leonard laughed, "Just kidding."

Lucy shook her head. "You're a mess, Leonard. You can't hide from me. I see the muddy side of your personality."

"How about we get rid of the mud, Lucy. I mean, literally, get rid of the mud."

"What?"

"Let me back the truck up and show you what I mean."

Lucy stepped aside as Leonard backed the truck up about five or so feet from the well opening. He turned off the engine, and hopped out, then walked back and opened the tailgate. "Okay, Lucy, let's pull this sucker out of the bed onto the ground."

Before Leonard could react, Lucy grabbed the crystal and yanked it almost out of the truck bed. He grabbed the other end, and they gently laid it on the ground.

"What now, Leonard?"

"Actually, I need a tripod, but we don't have one."

"Why a tripod?"

"I suspect that we could draw water if the negative side of this rock was pointed down, directly in the center of the well. The positive end of this thing was in the mud when we pulled it out. It's just a hunch, but I suspect that the positive end of the crystal cut off the flow."

"So, what now?"

"Let's roll the crystal up to the well so that the ends of it straddle the hole. Then we'll roll the crystal over the hole and see what happens. We'll position the positive pole toward the north."

The two set the crystal in place and then rolled it over the center of the hole. They looked in with a flashlight and waited. Nothing happened. They withdrew their gaze for a few minutes and looked back in. Nothing happened.

"Well! --- no pun intended. The mud's still there; life is a dead rock in a dead hole."

As the two reached to remove the crystal, Herk stood to attention and barked. Baba's fur stood straight up. A sound gurgled from the hole. Startled, they eased their gaze back into the well. Leonard turned on the light and pointed it down.

"My God, Leonard. The thing is filling up."

"Damn sure is! Uh, I guess I was wrong. Life is not a dead rock in a dead hole."

They watched and waited as the water rose in the well. As it was rising, they rolled the crystal back to the side of the well, and the water stopped its flow.

"Well! I'll be damned."

"Don't talk like that; don't damn yourself."

"Yeah, you're right, I'm just beside myself, Lucy." Leonard paused and took a breath. "Let's fill it to the brim."

Again, they rolled the crystal over the center of the well, waited and watched, as the water bubbled up to the brim; then they rolled the crystal back to the side.

"Goodness," said Lucy, eyes wide open. "It works like a faucet." She then dipped her hands in the water and stirred it. "It's warm and clear as glass."

Leonard stood up and began to take off his clothes.

"What are you doing, Leonard?"

"The same thing you did with me back in Mt. Shasta, remember?"

"Yeah, I remember," said Lucy, standing up and stripping down. "It's going to be a tight fit, but let's do it."

The two moved the crystal aside, and Leonard slipped into the water and held out his hand for Lucy. She took it and entered the water beside him. A four-foot diameter accommodated both of them. Their bodies touched. Lucy held on to Leonard's neck and his arms spread out above the surface of the well to keep them both above the water. All this took place as Herk ran in circles around the well and barked.

Laughing, Lucy turned her attention to Herk. "Not enough room in here for you, boy. Go play with Baba." Then, grinning from ear to ear, and face to face with Leonard, she declared, "I've never felt any umph like this before."

"Neither have I!"

"I'd say we've discovered the fountain of youth!"

"Yeah, skinny-dipping in the fountain of youth!"

CHAPTER 21

Mirror story

As the day was drawing nigh, the couple were cooling down from a jog down a long dusty road. As their camper came into view, Lucy turned to Leonard. "I don't think we should let anyone in on our find."

"What about my friend, Jeff? He helped me pull the crystal out of the well. He heard the same weird stuff I heard back there: 'dig up and read, dig up and read'."

"I wouldn't tell my own close friends right away, including Angel."

"Okay, why not?"

"Because of all the weird stuff that's happening. We know we have a crystal, one that pulls up water from a dry well. I know there's a lot of fuss over these stones – especially the large ones. They can be very valuable. Stones of value often attract the wrong crowd. We don't need to let the word get out right now. You need to give it more time and find out what's going on."

"Okay," said Leonard, in a slow thoughtful manner.

"You buy property, that was once a field, but now a wooded area. You find what might be a treasure in that area and don't know for sure its value. Is its value monetary or something else? I suspect that the value of your find is not about money; its value is something we can't see clearly right now. It might just be what Jay was talking about finding."

"I'm listening."

"There's more interesting stuff in your story, Leonard. There's a mirror in your story; it is the reverse image of a story found in the Gospel; I believe *Matthew*. A man finds a treasure in a field; he hides it, goes and sells everything he has, and buys that field. What he finds is not about money. The man in the story knows what he's found and hides it; you don't know what you've found, and you already own the property. Someone else might just come along and find the treasure, know its worth, and sell everything he has to buy it."

"I like that, Lucy, and this I know: you're a treasure."

Lucy gave Leonard an elbow in the ribs and winked; "You're a diamond in the rough."

"Let's go to work then."

CHAPTER 22

A WORMHOLE OF WATER

Within a week, with the assistance of a skid loader, Lucy and Leonard finished clearing the land around what was left of the log ruin. They set the logs aside and brought in more of the same. It was decided that the new structure would not be set in the same location or with the same rectangular shape, but directly over the spring. The couple agreed that the cabin would take the form of Angel's abode, not exactly a yurt, but a polygon consisting of twelve sides. The pitch of the roof was such that two people could walk up to the apex, remove a twelve-sided covering wrapped in metal roofing, and look directly down into the center of the cabin. The rafters would reflect the rays of the sun, circling around the structure and connecting up with a twelve-sided hoop at the apex. The floor of the building would be made of poplar, surrounding the exposed well. That's what they were working toward: a cabin that in no way resembled what had once dotted a bygone landscape. The most important part of this hybrid yurt would be the interior component placed directly over the well. Lucy and Leonard wanted to replicate a transducer-like component that would produce the same sound patterns shaped on the table in Angel's yurt. They wanted to build – not just any base and top -- but a base and top that served an acoustical purpose.

In a few weeks the building was up, but not trimmed out. The couple sat on the floor by the well with their feet dipped in it. They were discussing the next move when startled by the sound of footsteps outside the front entrance. Herk and Baba, napping near a back entrance, got up and moved to the door.

"Is it okay to come in? Am I disturbing anything?"

Leonard turned, stood up, and went to the door; it was his friend, Jeff, wearing short pants, a sweat shirt, and a pair of Sketcher's running shoes. He looked beat up.

"Jeff, where have you been?   Why haven't you answered my calls? I've missed you, buddy." The two hugged and stood back from each other. Leonard looked Jeff over and frowned. "Jeff, what the hell happened to your eye; that's a shiner! Is that a bandage on your head?"

Lucy appeared beside the two men and spoke up. "I've heard a lot about you Jeff, I'm Lucy." In a concerned manner, she asked, "Are you alright?"

"Frankly, no, I'm not." Jeff paused and answered Lucy. "Leonard did leave a message that he had a friend staying with him and that you guys were building a cabin. He wanted me to meet you, so here I am. What's left of me."

Lucy touched Jeff's shoulder, looked closely at his black eye, then softly spoke his name, "Jeff."

"I guess Leonard has told you about Betty."

"No. Who is Betty?"

"Betty is my wife. She's living with her personal trainer."

"That's got to be difficult," said Lucy.

"I'll just make a long story short. I got drunk, got pulled out of a tree and got my head split wide open. The next thing I knew was that I got the shit beat out of me. After that ordeal, I got sent to the emergency room to get stitches in my head.

They released me to a psyche ward to prevent me from hurting myself or killing the bastard that did this to me."

"What?" asked Leonard. "That doesn't sound like you. You've always been able to let things go, take your knocks and move on. I've never known anyone to kick your ass."

"Everyone has limits, Leonard, including you."

"How in the hell did you wind up in a tree?"

"I got drunk and went over to the trainer's house packing a 357 magnum and climbed a tree to watch and wait."

"Whose house are you talking about?" asked Lucy.

"The personal trainer's, my wife's lover. When they came out of the front door, I told Betty to stand back. He hid behind her, and she talked me into giving up the pistol. Then her personal trainer exercised his prowess; he yanked me out of the tree and beat me until I was dazed and almost unconscious, humiliating me in front of my wife. I can't sleep, can't eat, my head hurts, and my body aches. I can't even run to work off my pain, and there's no relief. That's what I've come to, Leonard, and someone needs killing!"

"No one needs killing, Jeff," said Lucy as she took his hand.

"Oh, yes, some people need a killing."

Jeff turned from the couple and moved to the center of the room. He pointed to the floor and remarked, "You've cut a hole in the floor." He peered over the edge into the well. "The damn thing is filled with water now." Turning to Leonard he asked, "Have you heard more strange voices?"

"Not since we pulled up that crystal."

"You still have it?"

"Yep."

Jeff hopped on the ground surrounding the well, then stooped and gently splashed the water. "It's warm and clear. You know, Leonard, you've got a great idea. You don't have to go outside to fetch your water."

"That's right; we built our kitchen centered on this spot. Look up, Jeff." Jeff turned his head to the center of the ceiling and saw the skylight letting light stream through.

"Nice," he said and continued, "Yep, perfect spot for an exhaust vent. Grill steaks and ribs in here anytime."

Jeff slipped off his socks and sneakers and dipped his feet into the warm water.

"Oh God," said Jeff, "that feels SOOO good."

The couple moved to the opening, sat down, and joined Jeff in what could have been a ceremonial foot washing.

Jeff removed the bandage from his head. Lucy, sitting to his right, could see the stitches.

"I want to clean the wound with your warm water," said Jeff.

Taking a clean paper cup, Lucy filled it with water and poured it on the wound.

"This is remarkable, guys; my headache is letting up!" As the other two looked on, Jeff removed his sweatshirt and slipped into the well. He went under the water and emerged. Laughing, he spoke of his action as a kind of baptism. "Now I know why folks flock to warm springs," said Jeff as he splashed water on his friends. "Leonard, are you sure you want a hut here? Hot springs sell."

"Wish we could join you, but the well is too small," smiled Lucy.

After a bit of friendly banter, Jeff tried to pull himself out of the well. The water level had dropped. Due to the water draining out of the well, Jeff called for Leonard to give him a hand. At the same time, Herk and Baba stirred around and burst from the hut.

Leonard bent down and grabbed Jeff's wrist struggling to get him out. Suddenly and unexpectedly, the water flushed out, as it swirled further and further downward. Their grip loosened, and Jeff fell into the rapidly draining darkness with the sound of a splash.

Leonard moved quickly to fetch a light and a rope. As Leonard lit up the hole, he and Lucy anxiously peered in. There was no sign of Jeff. But how could there be no Jeff when the bottom of the well appeared to be clear of mud and covered with rock?"

Over and over again, Lucy and Leonard called out, "Jeff!" The reply was only a slight echo.

CHAPTER 23

An OPEN SEWER

Leonard's eyes rolled; he shook his head and stared nervously around the room. "Oh, my God, what have we got ourselves into, Lucy?"

"What have you got us into?" snapped Lucy. "I'm calling 911."

"What? Hold up! Please put the phone down; give me a minute to think."

"There's no thinking to it, Leonard. Your friend's life is at stake! We need help now!"

Lucy dialed 9, and then a 1, and stopped. The sound of thunder rolled from the depths of the well. The couple watched in amazement as water rushed back into the well and filled it completely.

"It flushes and fills up again," said Leonard, "like a toilet."

"Yeah, but where is your friend? I don't see him. Turds don't flow backwards, Leonard. We need help, now!"

"Who's going to believe this? A man with mental issues disappears in a well with a solid bottom. Hell, I don't even believe it."

Lucy put her phone in her back pocket and quickly moved toward the front exit. She turned back to Leonard, "Are you coming?"

"Coming where?"

"Back to the camper."

As the two scurried back down the path, Herk darted out of the woods in front of them, barking his head off. He would not come to her on command, but stayed in place. Quickly, Lucy moved toward Herk. The couple watched as he backed into the woods. "Herk," called Lucy, "where is Baba?"

Herk backed into the brush and disappeared. The couple hurriedly followed behind. The dog led them to a huge sink hole.

"I never knew this was here," remarked Leonard, as they pushed the brush back and moved closer. What to their wondering eyes should appear at the bottom of the hole? Jeff was lying face up in a mud puddle with Baba on his chest. Before moving away, the cat appeared to be sniffing Jeff's nose. As the couple approached the body, not knowing if it was dead or alive, Jeff sprang straight up, like someone raising up out of an open coffin. He coughed up water, took a deep breath, looked around, and asked, "Where am I?"

CHAPTER 24

CROSSING INTO FORGETFULNESS

Early the next morning, Jeff got up and walked down the narrow hall to the front of the Airstream where Lucy and Leonard were sitting at the kitchen table over breakfast. With a look of sleepy surprise, he addressed Leonard and asked, "How did I get here at your place?"

"You ran here; your shorts and sweat shirt are in the dryer. Your sneakers are by the door. You were dehydrated. It's a good twenty miles to your house."

"I'm sorry, but I'm don't remember any run." Turning to Lucy, he asked, "You must be Leonard's friend, the one helping to build the cabin."

"Oh," said Leonard, "You got my message."

"Yeah, sure did, but I've been out of commission for a while in the hospital." Jeff pointed to the stitches on the side of his head and went on, "As you can see."

Lucy got up and grabbed a bottle of water from the fridge; Jeff, in the interval, had taken a seat when she returned and handed him the bottle.

"Thanks," he hesitated "You're…?"

"Lucy."

"Other than not remembering how I got here, I'm doing great. The bump on the head and the black eye came from falling out of a tree. Stitches fixed my head and several ECT treatments worked wonders. I got better after every treatment. In several days, I felt like my old self again, not overreacting to a loss. My wife is now my ex-wife. I've written her off, and I'm moving on."

"Your brain was shocked?" asked Lucy.

"Actually, it was convulsed. Don't believe the bad press; I mean, the disinformation on the subject. I'm missing a bit of upfront memory, but other than that, it's a miracle. Yeah, I'm good to go, ready to see what you guys have been working on."

Simultaneously, Lucy and Leonard looked at each other and turned back to Jeff. Leonard spoke up, "You came out here yesterday afternoon. We took you to see the cabin." They were silent and waited for a response.

"Honestly, Leonard, I only remember waking up." With a burst of energy, Jeff continued, "Take me to your building project."

"Yeah, sure, Jeff."

Lucy chimed in, "Let's do it!"

When they arrived at the yurt-like structure, with its twelve-sided walls and pointed roof, Jeff stopped in his tracks and looked in amazement. "You guys, did it. The thing is spectacular!" Addressing Lucy, he asked, "Are you the architect?"

"No." smiled Lucy, "U-tube and books taught us what to do."

After walking into the structure, Jeff looked up and marveled at the rafters as they converged onto a hub at the apex of the roof. Looking down, he noticed the well filled with water, and quickly praised Leonard for bringing the cabin to the well. "I can visualize a kitchen counter right over this well, with a sink and an old-fashioned built-in grill right beside it, steaks and ribs anytime."

Toward evening, Leonard drove his friend back to his house. Before getting out of the truck, Jeff turned to Leonard. "I'm glad that you're back and that I could sell you the property. I'm glad you met Lucy. She's good for you; I appreciate being at the right place at the right time, your listening ear, and Lucy's. Now, I'm looking forward to getting back to work."

"And thank you for being a friend. You be safe, Jeff."

CHAPTER 25

THE BACK BURNER

Lucy slept an hour late the next morning. When she woke up, she moved slowly into the kitchen area, sat down with Leonard at the kitchen table, closed her eyes, and rested her finger tips on her head. Without looking up, she asked Leonard for a warm cup of water. No words followed as Leonard warmed the water and gently placed the cup before her.

"Are you alright, Lucy?"

Lucy opened her eyes. "No, my muscles cramped last night; I felt dizzy, but couldn't go to sleep. I just lay there, trying to think, but couldn't."

"That's what pain relievers are for."

"I know." Several moments of silence followed and Lucy continued. "I owe you an apology, Leonard."

"You owe me an apology. For what?"

"I freaked the other day when Jeff went under the water and disappeared. I blamed you for 'getting us into the situation'."

"I don't remember, Lucy. Anyway, it's no biggie. Let it go."

"No, I can't let it go. We have found ourselves in a quandary."

"I'm afraid I don't understand. What is the quandary?"

"Well, Leonard, it puzzles me how Jeff came over despondent, went through a tunnel of water, and woke up to an entirely different story, one with a more positive outlook. He talked about a memory loss. It must have been from the shock treatments he underwent. He changed his mind about killing people. In fact, he joked about having a baptism and how the water helped his pain. Other than that, I find it hard to believe that Jeff was sucked into a well and came out somewhere else."

"Yeah," replied Leonard, "and not remembering where it was or how he got there. Jeff heard the whispers before I did, 'dig up and read'."

"Stones don't whisper, Leonard."

"Then what's your take on this perplexing situation?"

"Honestly, I don't know what to think. Maybe we should let Jeff in on what he doesn't remember. After all, he doesn't recall having been sucked down in the well and then coming up with what appears to be a new outlook."

"Maybe so," Lucy.

"Let's put it on the back burner for now. Jeff's mind seems scrambled. We'll have our opportunity to open the door later."

CHAPTER 26

A METAPHYSICAL PLUMBER

The plumber looked familiar, but Leonard couldn't quite place who he was. The man stooped down beside the toilet bowl and looked in. The bowl was empty and stained. Then, the plumber gave it a flush. Leonard was looking over the man's shoulder as the two watched the bowl fill up with dirty water.

"It's not supposed to do that," said Leonard.

"This is not a physical leak," replied the man, continuing to stare downward into the bowl. "You've got a backflow, a metaphysical backflow."

"How do you fix it?"

"I can't fix it."

"I don't understand. That's what plumber's do."

"I'm on the wrong side of the flow" he replied. "A plunger or a snake won't work from this side. I'm a metaphysical plumber, on the wrong side of the problem."

"Who do I call?"

"You don't have to call anyone from your side; you don't even need a plunger or a snake. Watch, I'll show you what I mean."

Still looking over the man's shoulder, Leonard watched as the plumber flushed the toilet. Filthy water filled the bowl and began to swirl, but would not empty. The dirtiness of the water turned into a picture of a stormy day after a rain. A Confederate soldier was looking up through toilet water but appeared not see the other side; he seemed trapped in another dimension."

"There's the problem: that's Johnny Reb. He's caught in the plumbing – flowing in the wrong direction – I suspect that he wants to flow back and fight again."

"Fight again?" asked Leonard. "What the hell are you talking about?"

"The sucker's looking for a rebirth. He wants to come back and, I believe, fight the Civil War again."

The two continued to stare into the bowl. They watched as the bowl's rim morphed into the face of a compass. A crystal appeared and turned in the direction of north. They observed the Confederate turn his attention to the crystal, and he slowly moved toward it. His dirty hands fondled the crystal. He tried to move it, but his hands moved ghost-like through the stone.

"There's your problem – a metaphysical one. We've got a temporary fix, but we've got to redirect the flow. Call me back when you set things in place." The plumber turned around, winked, and vanished.

Leonard woke up, opened his eyes, and realized that Jay was the plumber who had come to him in a dream. Leonard stayed in the bed for some time thinking about the dream and the shadowy metaphysical plumber.

Thinking about Lucy, Leonard got up and moved down the hall to Lucy's bed. Softly, he asked, "Lucy, are you awake?"

"Yes, I'm awake."

"May I snuggle with you?"

"Yes, I'd like that." Lucy pulled back the cover. Leonard glimpsed her nakedness in the early morning light, then slipped in beside her. She drew near him, and he held her close in his arms.

"That's nice," she said.

"Yes, it is. You bring a new way of experiencing the world. I don't want it to end; I don't want to mess it up."

"Neither do I, Leonard. I don't want you to see my weaknesses and walk away."

"I feel the same way. I fear your seeing my weaknesses and feeling humiliated, like Jeff."

The couple were silent for some time, resting in their embrace. Leonard kissed her forehead, then spoke. "If you feel weak, I want to be strong for you – no white lies or noble lies – just the truth. You don't have to hold anything back from me; I promise, I will not let go of you."

"I'll remember that promise," said Lucy. She drew closer, placed her hands against his face, and kissed him on the lips.

CHAPTER 27

ACOUSTICAL TRANSFORMATION

After Lucy left for a doctor's appointment at 10 o'clock, Leonard walked back to the cabin. Thinking what most people would think, that the dream had a message, he entered the cabin, hopped down off the floor beside the well and began to maneuver the crystal. He took a compass from his shirt pocket and made an effort to locate north; the needle spun erratically. So, Leonard left the cabin to get an accurate reading. Returning to the cabin, he lined the positive pole of the crystal between a section of wall that he determined to be north. He gazed into the well and waited, but nothing happened.

Herk and Baba appeared at the door. Leonard watched as they moseyed about the place, moving through an assortment of portable electric tools. It was time to prepare for a day of work. Leonard walked just outside the cabin, in the direction of a portable generator, when Herk and Baba came to attention. Both darted out of the cabin and went down the path, stopped, and looked back. Leonard felt a vibration and heard the sound of a distant roar; the vibration and the roar increased until the earth shook. The commotion culminated in a muffled boom from under the cabin and was quiet again.

Herk and Baba looked up at Leonard as if to ask, "What are you waiting for?" Leonard strolled back to the well and looked down. Clear water boiled up but did not overflow; it appeared to flow back down into the ground.

Working throughout the day, Leonard noticed that the sounds coming from his skill saw and drill were amplified, and then reverberated. When he whistled a tune, the dog howled and the cat purred. There was a change that produced an acoustical transformation that changed the experience in the room.

CHAPTER 28

RISKING TO TELL THE TRUTH

Leonard had just finished feeding the pets when Lucy returned from seeing the doctor. He watched as Lucy approached the door carrying a bag of groceries in one hand. Leonard opened the door and took the groceries.

"Anything else to bring in?" he asked.

"No, that's it," she said. "You might want to turn on the local news."

"What's up?"

"The weather service reported seismic activity this morning in our area. Did you feel any tremor?"

"Sure did."

Lucy turned to Leonard with a look of surprise and gave him a peck on the cheek. "Tell me about it."

"Later," said Leonard. "Tell me how your day went."

"They ran a blood test. The good news is that my blood panel remains the same. Other than that, I feel much better."

"I appreciate your telling me this."

"It's the truth, Leonard. I was born with one kidney, and I need to be careful not to put it under undue stress. I grew up frail; it made me feel like a runt. Music and the outdoors

84

became my obsession. I love to play the guitar, and I love to sweat; I love to feel good and look good."

Leonard smiled. "I love your sweat and crave your music; they show your soul and magnify something?"

"And what might that something be?"

"That you're drop-dead good looking!"

Lucy gently placed her arms around Leonard's neck, "You're special."

"Lucy, we will get through this."

CHAPTER 29

VALIS: VAST ACTIVE LIVING INTELLIGENT SOUL

Leonard spoke up, "You'll just have to see it to believe it."

"Why don't we bring our guitars to the well and listen," said Lucy.

"Why not?"

Carrying camp chairs and their guitars, the two made their way to the cabin. Upon entering, Lucy hurried to the well and looked down from the edge of the floor.

"My God, Leonard, it's boiling just like the water under Angel's cabin." Leonard looked on as Lucy gazed in amazement and exclaimed, "What a coincidence!"

Suddenly, they heard a voice coming from the entrance. "It is no coincidence, young lady, call it a meaningful occurrence." The two turned and saw the shadow of a figure who was standing there blocking the sunlight. The figure moved closer in the shadow.

"Jesus!" blurted Lucy. "You're supposed to be dead."

"Well, here I am," said Jay. "No, I'm not Jesus, and I'm not dead. The soul never dies. I'm yours truly, in the spirit."

"Really, Jay, is that you?" asked Lucy.

"Believe it or not, it's me."

"My God!" declared Leonard. "It is him!"

"No, Leonard, I am not your God, just an older version of my earthly self. I'm an old soul."

Lucy and Leonard stepped back. Gesturing to the couple, Jay held his palms out. "You guys don't have to be afraid; I don't have COVID. Come over here and give me a hug."

Jay took a step forward, and the couple slowly approached him. "It is you," said Lucy.

Jay held his arms out and Leonard responded, reluctantly, and then stepped back.

Looking Leonard in the eye, Jay spoke. "I told you I'd catch up with you. I presume you received the package."

Leonard nodded, "Yeah, the Phillip Dick book, *VALIS*.

"Did you read it?"

"Yes, I did."

"So, Leonard, what does VALIS stand for?"

"As I recall, VAST ACTIVE LIVING INFORMATION SYSTEM."

"That's why I'm here to introduce you to a conceptual upgrade. On a three-D level we can refer to it as an informational system. On the quantum or multidimensional level, we're dealing with an intelligent soul: a VAST ACTIVE LIVING INTELLIGENT SOUL. God's throne is in a superposition, meaning through HIM all things are possible. Through this power, creation evolves; it's open-ended, not closed, as in a system."

"Let me see if I've got this right. You're talking about the World Soul," said Lucy.

"You're getting warm, Lucy. Take another crack."

"Living and active."

"You're getting warmer."

"How about, 'aware of Itself' or 'self-awareness'?"

"Push further, Lucy."

Finally, Lucy asked, "Could superposition and super coherence say something about the nature of this intelligent soul?"

"It does. This coherent soul possesses memory and imagination; it is creative and active; it actively brings stuff into being with and without the need of a craftsman."

"Can this intelligent being become a human, something like a craftsman?"

"Yes, Lucy."

Leonard interrupted, "You're saying this VALIS stepped aside and became human?"

"Yes, I'm saying that VALIS became human, but he didn't exactly *step aside* or *come off a high throne* in order to craft things from stuff. Human beings are more than mere stuff. Human beings do not come into being as complete packages. They are co-creators with VALIS, not automatons.

"And why would he do that?" asked Leonard. "Humans act like automatons. The world is totally screwed. Folks are living in the presence of a VALBS – A VAST ACTIVE LIVING BABBLED SYSTEM. People are spreading lies and disinformation in high places to serve whom? Themselves."

"And, you're right, Leonard. Many are called and few are receptive. This puts some people at the end of their vocabularies, with nothing to peddle but lies, cliches and platitudes. Isn't that where you are, Leonard, at the end of your vocabulary, looking for a little help from friends? You do have the freedom to reach beyond yourself." Jay turned to Lucy. "And you want to believe the lie that you're not pretty. You want to believe that all men have VALBS souls. You can choose otherwise. VALIS stepped off his throne in the sense that humans might transcend this unfortunate condition. His/her emotional makeup is in perfect harmony. (S)He can love and forgive through empathy. Humans can choose to attain this harmony, not by worshiping a Being who stepped off a high place, but stepped into the personal lives of others

88

with compassion and mercy. You are made in the image of God and can do the same. You can fully engage an intersubjective world and experience joy. What the world fails to realize is that existence is not centered in matter. 'Flesh and blood do not inherit the Kingdom of God.' Existence or life is Spirit-centered. The essence of VALIS is not manufactured or crafted by human hands."

Lucy and Leonard stood there listening, taking it all in, as if knowing that they had no comeback.

Jay changed the subject. "Okay, guys, faith relies on testimony; reason relies not just on evidence and examination, but on the lived experience. Do what you both came here to do: test out the sound system and see how it works."

The couple took out their guitars and set the camp chairs in place. They were about to begin when Jay directed each of them to sit on opposite sides of the well. They took their designated places. Lucy, the more accomplished player, started with their favorite composer, Tárrega. She began with a piece familiar to Leonard, *Adelita*, then moved to the *Capricho Árabe*, a serenata. The movement concluded with *Recuerdos De La Alhambra*. They had never played these pieces together because the music was virtuoso material, not at all manageable for a duet. Lucy had memorized all three pieces while Leonard had only memorized the first two and only parts of the final piece. Lucy played through the two verses, and Leonard did the same. Through the second piece, they began to play together and improvise, drawing notes from some unknown place. The final piece began with Lucy playing the top part, while Leonard played the bottom line; then they continued as before in a melody that blended the composition, without losing the beauty of it.

The music stopped. The two were silent for a while gazing at one another from across the well, as if waiting to come down from an intoxication. "I don't remember anything," said Lucy, "only the experience of being one with divine music. I felt myself spinning, not out of control, but somehow in Leonard's space."

"At first," said Leonard, "the music took my breath away. I, too, felt myself spinning, round and round, faster and faster, in Lucy's space. Her hands and heart became mine, moving perfectly, touching strings I'd never reached before."

"Good!" exclaimed Jay. "Now, you both are on training wheels. Thanks to the crystal and its location, you've both magnified your vibrational level. Now that you've got a foretaste of things to come, I've got to make haste. Be careful how you use your advantage."

Jay walked over to the well, turned to the couple and made a final remark. "Whatever you do, don't do what I'm about to do. Keep out of the water. I'll catch you guys later." At that, Jay jumped in feet first and disappeared under the bubbles.

CHAPTER 30

THE MIDDLE REGION

The following week, Jay emerged out of the well while Lucy and Leonard were practicing duets. After Jay hoisted himself up, the couple watched as the water evaporated off of him. "Hi, guys," said Jay, smiling. Jay looked his body over, and continued. "The frequency is out of sync. You've still got a plumbing problem."

"Out of sync?" questioned Lucy.

"Yep, water doesn't evaporate off a spiritual body; water takes the shape of a spiritual body in or out of the water." Jay took on a serious look accompanied by a momentary pause. "Under the circumstances, my time is limited. You guys need to listen up. Astronauts get briefed and trained before going into outer space; you guys need a briefing before taking a venture into inner space. Don't ask any questions; just look and listen."

Jay directed his friends to look over into the well. Under the clear water was the ghost-like dirty-handed Confederate soldier that Leonard had seen in his dreamlike experience in the lava tube. At the time, the soldier was dead and had been thrown over into the well. Now, he was animated, looking up at the crystal, caressing it and attempting to push it aside. When he tried to move the stone, the crystal lit up and those dirty hands melted into the object.

"Imagine a coin," said Jay. "It has two sides and a middle. There's clarity on both sides of the coin: heads and tails. You have to turn the coin over to see the other side; you can't see through the coin to the other side. The coin has a middle region. Using the coin as an analogy, the Confederate soldier is stuck in the middle region between dimensions. You want to avoid going into that middle region; it's a region of transition, where chaos and turbulence occur. You saw it on Angel's acoustic table as tones changed their shape. There must be a clear region between the inner and outer side of these dimensions in order to glimpse through it. To extend the analogy, heads and tails of a coin are like electron shells. Electrons never cross the gap – the middle region -- they merely appear and disappear from one shell to the other. If the mind is clear, seeing is like that. If the path is clear, one simply sees across the gap. No crossing is necessary. Now, going from one acoustic state to another takes the process a step further. At that point, it is possible for the object or body to materialize in different forms."

Jay continued, "In this case, I have what you would call a spiritual body, not entirely unlike your own spiritual body. You guys are just at the starting line; you have to choose whether or not to move any further. If you do, then continue with your project by constructing a bed over the well. When that is completed, you can sleep on it. Under these physical conditions, you will transition from delta sleep to acoustic consciousness. The vibrational level of this state enables your spiritual form to time travel and even enter the informational matrices of others, both living and dead. At some point, you can even enter the lived experiences of these people. For now, you will be able to stand back and view the Confederate soldier's story. This idea of remote viewing is a military term. This procedure gives you the advantage of finding out how and why he got trapped in the well and why this information is important to you. Don't rush the process, be patient. *Once* again, don't ever do what I'm about to do! Got to go." Jay quickly turned and jumped back into the well, feet first.

CHAPTER 31

Toxic soap

The tops of the tall trees were beginning to turn green when Lucy and Leonard completed putting the fiberglass doors and casement windows in the cabin. The place had been wired for solar, was insulated, and drywall was ready for finishing. The weather was sunny and warm and the evenings cool and refreshing.

"Spring brings out the wild woman in me," declared Lucy. "I want to get naked and run through the woods -- just run and run and run until my body is drenched, and it feels so good."

"Sounds good to me," said Leonard, grinning. Hurriedly, he threw off his tee shirt and dropped his pants. Lucy followed suit, and they were off and running, wearing only their trail shoes, following a circular path made by local hunters. They were circling the cabin over and over again, until they were breathless and drenched in sweat. On the final lap, they did not cool off, but hurried into the cabin. The casement windows were open, and they could feel an incoming breeze touch the sweat that covered them.

"What a tension release!" shouted Leonard. "I love it."

"It feels so good – down and dirty – outright sexy, Leonard."

"Shame on you, naughty girl," said Leonard, laughing.

"Yes, I am a naughty girl. You need to wash down these impurities that cling to this dirty flesh."

Leonard stepped down from the floor by the well carrying an empty five-gallon bucket and dipped it into the water. He stood up and looked at Lucy. "Get down here, girl, and bring the soap."

Lucy picked up the soap, stepped down, and dropped it to the ground. Leonard poured the warm spring water over her head, slowly, and watched the water flow down her trim, muscular and fit body.

"Do it again!" she shouted. "Fill it up and do it again!"

Leonard did it again and watched her response. Lucy's eyes rolled in delight. She spread out her arms and crooned, "It feels so good." She opened her eyes and quickly stepped up onto the floor. Leonard handed her a full bucket of water, and she proceeded to pour it over his head, slowly, and watched as it flowed down his body. "Now, you naughty boy, pick up the soap and lather me down."

They took turns with the soap, almost in an embrace. When both were fully covered in white lather, they were interrupted, startled, by the sound of water splashing up and out of the well.

"I'm back," said Jay, looking up and holding onto the edge of the well. Their guest panicked, and it wasn't because he caught them in the buck. "I hope you guys aren't planning to jump in!"

"Now, why would we do that when you told us not to, not once but twice?" asked Lucy.

"Oh, good." Jay breathed a sigh of relief and continued to probe. "You guys didn't sip or drink the water, did you?"

"No, Jay, we did not consume any of the water, but we did get wet with it," said Leonard, pointing to the five-gallon bucket by the well's edge.

Jay gave another sigh of relief. "That's not so bad, but that water isn't going to take off all that soap you're lathered in. This well water is downright toxic."

"Really," said Leonard, taking the bucket, filling it, then pouring water over Lucy and himself.

"Told you so, but no worry; tap water will take it off."

Jay pulled himself up out of the well and sat down on the floor in a half-lotus position. Lucy and Leonard did the same.

"I'm a spiritual being having a physical experience, so, listen up because, as ever, I don't have much time. You guys don't have to cover this well like Angel did over his well in Mt. Shasta. He's caught up in cymatics: patterns made by sound. These patterns aren't going to cleanse this well. You guys need to cover this whole area with a bed and sleep on it. Start living over here."

"It's that simple?" questioned Leonard. "Just sleep on it, and the problem will go away?"

"Look back into the well," said Jay.

Lucy and Leonard peered into the water and, again, they saw the ghost of a Confederate soldier.

"This Reb is imprisoned down there, and he wants to get loose. We need to watch his history and find out if the guy is worth setting free. Then, and only then, will we be able to determine his fate," said Jay. "You may not want to deliver him to your back yard."

"Then, what do we do next?" asked Lucy.

"Just sleep on the bed. After that, there's no turning back. I'll see you in your dreams. Remember, you'll be spiritual persons having a physical experience."

Abruptly, Jay got up and jumped back into the well, feet first.

CHAPTER 32

DREAMING

One man, on horseback, dismounted at the edge of a freshly plowed field. The other, catching sight of the first, brought the mule to a halt and laid down the plow. Not hurrying, they walked toward one another, shook hands, and embraced.

"Good to see you, brother. It's been a spell."

"It's good to see you, Tom. I see you've improved the old homestead."

"Yeah, we're happy here, plan to make it a permanent home."

"That's nice, Tom, but there's a war going on."

"I heard about you getting rich in Memphis. Didn't think that a high flutter like you could take such quick note of my correspondence."

"Well, I did and that's why I rode all this way to recruit you. I'm a lieutenant colonel now, and I raised a battalion of 650 mounted troopers. We'll soon be headed out to Kentucky. We're going to have a heap of fun killing yanks. I need a man I can trust who can ride and shoot. You're that man, Tom."

"Nate, I'm not about this war. I got a young girl -- she's blind as a bat -- but she's the prettiest thing you've ever seen. Brother, I want to stay home and nibble on her titties."

"I would like to see this pretty gal you talked about in that most extraordinary letter."

Nate took the reins of his horse, and the two moseyed up to the old homeplace, a small, one-room log cabin. They walked in and Nate saw the girl stirring a pot of beans she'd prepared for the noon meal. Nate stood stone cold still with his gaze fixed on the blind girl. "I'm not believing this," he said.

The blind girl walked over to Nate and made a clicking sound. "I recognize you, too, Mr. Forrest."

Tom turned to Nate. "You know her?"

"Yep, I do. She's the blind mulatto girl form Arkansas – got a high dollar for her on the block – eyes so pretty you'd think she could see with them."

"She sees by making clicking sounds, Nate."

"I know." Nate addressed the girl, "I remember selling you to a banker in College Grove, don't remember his name."

"His name was John Cromer," said the girl.

"Oh, yes, I remember, Cromer."

Slowly, Nate turned his attention to Tom and spoke, "Do you know what or who you're living with? Tom, how did you get yourself into this affair?"

"I came to the farmer's market one morning and saw Cromer slap this blind girl to the ground. Something came over me to stick up for her. I got stiff in my britches and knocked Cromer to the ground. He reached for his pistol and fired one shot that grazed my earlobe. I returned fire before he could get off another shot; the bullet took half his head off."

"I can't believe you took up for a half-nigger. That was his property, Tom."

"Not anymore. A dead man doesn't own any property."

"Mr. Forrest," said the blind girl, "your brother picked this half-nigger off the ground after that killing. You know what he said to me?"

"I can't imagine," said Nate. "Tell me."

The blind girl replied, "Tom said, 'I'm lonely enough to kill a fool over you. How about you? Are you lonely enough to love that kind of man?'" She paused and continued, "I reached out and touched his face, then took his hands and saw into his soul. Your brother, Mr. Forrest, is a good man. I was lonely enough to say 'yes,' because he saw me as something other than chattel."

The girl's distinct accent was not southern. It must have jogged Forrest's memory. "You have a reputation for trouble," snapped Nate, "ever since you came up from the islands – practicing voodoo. If you didn't hold my little brother in such a spell, I'd shoot your black ass on the spot."

"Hold up, Nate, compose yourself!" shouted Tom, as he stepped between the two.

The blind girl spoke up, "If you know my reputation, Mr. Forrest, you know that I have the means to see all the way from Arkansas to Kentucky, so let's cut to the chase – do a deal that will rise you in rank overnight and make you a legend. That's what you want, isn't it?"

"Sounds like a pact with the devil," quipped Forrest. "I'm interested in taking the Yankee government out of the South."

"Here's the deal, Mr. Forrest. There's a crystal with special powers buried in Arkansas. You bring it to me on your way to Kentucky, and you'll have the information needed to face your foe. Just leave Tom here; give him a uniform if you want, and call this place a battalion outpost." With that, the girl moved across the room and removed a map from a dresser drawer. She returned, then handed the paper to Forrest. He looked at it and tucked it inside the pocket of his gray jacket and said, "I'll think about it."

CHAPTER 33

Fʀᴏᴍ ARKANSAS TO KENTUCKY

Nathan Bedford Forrest didn't give it much thought at all. He, 'the Gray Ghost,' and his entourage galloped to Arkansas for the purpose of retrieving the stone. When the mission was accomplished, the battalion headed to Kentucky. Crossing through Tennessee, Forrest and a handful of his confederates broke from the group and detoured toward the outpost.

"I can see them now, Tom," said the blind girl. "They're coming today."

Early that afternoon several soldiers appeared at the doorstep of the cabin. On the small square bed of a buck board wagon rested the crystal covered by a tarp. Forrest dismounted and uncovered the five-foot crystal, an elongated, six-sided, clear gemstone. Five men easily carried it into the cabin and sat it horizontally on two hand hewn logs which were about knee high. Forrest, carrying a package, motioned his men to leave and handed his brother the bundle.

Watching Tom open the wrapping, Forrest spoke to his brother: "You are officially in the service of the Army of the Confederate States. You hold the rank of sergeant; this post is your charge."

Looking down at the contents of the package, Tom replied, "Nate, I love you brother, but I don't want this uniform."

"Do you want the Federal government telling you what you can and can't do?"

"Of course, I don't! And I don't want your government to tell me that my wife is a piece of property."

"I'm not arguing with you. We've made a deal, so let's get on with it." Forrest, turned to the blind girl. "So, what's so special about the stone?"

"It's funny, Mr. Forrest, that everyone – especially you – knows what's so special about this stone. The problem is that you just don't remember. It's humorous that you travel all the way to Arkansas to fetch the stone because some hidden memory takes you there. This memory dwells on the tip of your tongue, but you just can't spit it out."

"Well, spit it out for me -- jog my declining memory!"

"As they say, Mr. Forrest, *knowledge is power*. Knowledge is nothing more than information. You need information to win the war. I suspect that you'll do whatever it takes to get it. You don't realize that the real war is within yourself."

"So, what the hell has that got to do with the stone?"

"Direct your attention to the stone, Mr. Forrest. Look into it. What do you see?"

Forrest looked into the crystal. "I don't see a thing, nothing but clear glass."

"Now, touch it with both hands and keep your hands in place. Read the text, Mr. Forrest. It's there."

"Voodoo lady, this is bull shit! I don't see a damn thing!"

The blind girl rested her palms on the back of Forrest's hands. Suddenly, Forrest's eyes opened wide. He gave out a gasp and quickly pulled his hands off the stone, and then turned to the blind girl and shouted. "You're the devil!"

"No, Mr. Forrest, I am not the devil. You've been provided information. What you choose to do with that information is not only your choice, but your responsibility. Take care to choose wisely, Mr. Forrest, because somewhere down the line, you will reap what you've sown. That said, you may, in fact, be in pact with the devil himself. I suspect that you will return, again and again, living in forgetfulness and looking for the Arkansas crystal."

CHAPTER 34

DREAMS WITHIN DREAMS

Lucy opened her eyes, got out of bed and dressed. Leonard was sleeping soundly on the bed they'd placed over the well's opening. It was dark outside. Lucy walked out into the open air in the presence of a clear starry sky. Moonlight filled the air with a silvery glow. A figure emerged from the path. Recognizing the figure, she smiled. "Oh, what a pleasant surprise. I thought you were in LA."

"Listen up, Lucy," said Jay. "You can blink, but don't close your eyes. Your brain is in deep sleep. You're in a place where dreams are not thought to take place, and you're about to experience remote viewing in multiple dimensions. Now, turn around."

Lucy turned around. The cabin that she and Leonard had built was no longer there. Night turned into day. She found herself standing on the back side of the ruin. The landscape was not the same, not as full, but full enough to be considered a wooded area. On one side of the cabin, she beheld a side-car motorcycle, much like the one Leonard had recently acquired. She recognized that a platform had been built over well. She and Jay watched as a man wearing jodhpurs and knee boots mounted the stand and assumed a lotus position. With his arms resting on his knees palms up, he closed his eyes.

"Lucy," said Jay, "that's a military man, a remote viewer, looking for an advantage, and he's found his target."

"And what is that target?"

"He's sitting on top of the well where the crystal is hidden. There's one problem; he's viewed a dead rock, meaning there's no advantage from the crystal due to its orientation in the well. His advantage comes from where he's sitting, on top of an energy node. Also, he can't lay hands on the crystal because he's not there, in the flesh, to fish it up. Right now, he can only look backwards; he can even simulate a three-dimensional appearance, but he can't look forward. The guy in the knee boots is located in Germany right before WWII. Do you recognize him?"

"No, I don't. Who is he?"

"The Desert Fox."

"You mean, General Erwin Rommel, the WWII Field Marshall commanding a tank division through France and on to Northern Africa."

"Bingo!"

"So, what's he doing?"

"Let's watch, Lucy. I suspect he'll disappear."

They waited a bit, then watched as the German disappeared in front of their eyes.

"He's bilocated," said Jay. "Let's step up on the platform and try to sync into his location."

Taking a position on the platform, Lucy spoke up. "Yes, I see the location, a small town on bluffs overlooking the Tennessee River. I see a sign over a store, Clifton Mercantile. A ferry is crossing the river. The traffic gives it the look of the nineteen-thirties. There's a side-car motorcycle parked on the street. At the end of the street is a lovely home with a wrap-around porch. I see a lady on the porch in a swing. She's talking with Rommel in German. She walks back into the house. He takes her seat in the swing and looks across the yard, past the side-car motorcycle. Gazing on the river, he closes his eyes."

"That's our cue, Lucy. Now, take Rommel's place on the swing and watch."

"It looks like the Civil War era," said Lucy, fixing her gaze. "There are no cars or trucks, only wagons and horses. I see the same ferry crossing the river as well as a grand riverboat. There is the sound of a banjo coming from the boat. The town appears to be bustling and filled with more people than we just saw. I see the German observing a ranking Confederate officer. The Confederates are in great number, and they are building flatboats along the riverbank. The officer seems like someone I've seen before, but I can't place him."

"That officer is Nathan Bedford Forrest, Lucy. Rommel is studying Forrest's military maneuvers. I suspect that Rommel will bilocate all through Tennessee." She and Jay were silent for several seconds.

"It's time to go," said Jay, "before we get lost in the layers."

Lucy and Jay stepped down from the platform. After turning around 180 degrees, they were back in front of the cabin where Lucy had stepped into the waking dream. It was still nighttime when the two entered the cabin. Lucy looked in on herself, sleeping soundly beside Leonard. As she closed her eyes, she saw Jay take Leonard on the same tour.

CHAPTER 35

Reunited

When Lucy and Leonard woke up, the sun was shining through the surrounding casement windows. Jay scurried about in the kitchen area preparing breakfast on a propane camp stove; the smell of sausage and eggs filled the room. The couple dressed, slipped on shoes, and walked out to relieve themselves, then returned and seated themselves at a makeshift table. Jay placed three plates of breakfast on the table. The couple looked at each other, then turned to Jay with questioning expressions.

Knowing what was on their minds, Jay nonchalantly remarked, "Yes, some spiritual beings eat. Enjoy, guys."

"You must be a hungry ghost," remarked Lucy.

"Jay looked up from his plate. "Call me a hungry ghost, but just remember that I'm not here to do you harm."

"You're not going to duck out on us, are you?" questioned Leonard.

"Oh, no! Not at all. I have time to spend. The plumbing problem isn't at all what it could have been. It's an easy fix. We'll take care of it after breakfast. Eat up guys."

Taking a mouthful of scrambled eggs, Leonard looked across the table at their guest and asked, "Jay, who are you? Why are you doing this?"

"Yeah, Jay," echoed Lucy. "You don't seem like the same person I knew last year. You look the same, but come across differently"

"Good question, guys." Jay sipped his coffee and went on. Back about the time you guys were growing up, I had a talk with my immediate supervisor. He gave me an assignment, to reincarnate and find two compatible and teachable souls. You two were the match. So, when that part of the assignment was finished, I checked back in. You guys think that I checked out."

"So, what do you teach?" asked Lucy.

"Do you want the long version or the short?"

Leonard interjected, "Just spit it out, Jay."

"I simply teach folks how to live in their transient world. The method is not about what to think, but how to think. Also, you've got to get out of the way and allow your consciousness to be in alignment with VALIS. It's not that easy because your autonomic nervous system has to be aligned with a higher frequency. Such is not entirely within one's conscious control. Training wheels short circuit all that, but true coherence comes with time and without a crutch."

"Doesn't thinking and acting not have an important part to play in consciousness?" asked Leonard.

"Of course, it does," replied Jay. "We live in a unified field of information. Right now, your thoughts and acts aren't in the right relationship to that field." Jay paused and looked directly at Leonard. "For one who had come to the end of his vocabulary, you may not believe that this field even exists."

"If you're talking about God, I believe in the possibility of God," said Leonard.

107

"Yeah, you believe in the possibility of many things, but you do not have a conviction strong enough to change your habits. That's why the training wheels."

"I don't see these training wheels."

"Oh, you've seen these wheels, Leonard. It's the crystal that enables you to bridge between two planes of experience. What has been referred to as the implicate and explicate orders of reality.

After breakfast the three placed their dirty dishes in a five-gallon bucket of water. Leonard and Lucy rolled the bed away so as to reveal the well. The three of them looked down from the floor. They could clearly see the Confederate's face, looking up, motioning them, as if to say, "Come on in."

Turning to Leonard, Jay asked. "Does that guy look familiar?"

"Yes, yes, he sure does! That's the guy in my dream last night. He's also the guy I saw on the wall of the lava tube. That's Tom, Nathan Forrest's little brother."

"How did he get down in there?"

"A Yank ran a sword through him. Before his soul could leave the body, the body was dumped into the well along with the crystal."

"That's right, Leonard. He's been stuck down there ever since, wandering around in that middle region, giving off toxins of despair. What else do you recognize about this fellow?"

"Well, he took up for a blind girl and loved her, despite the color of her skin. He killed in self-defense. Really, I thought well of him." Leonard paused to gather his thoughts and continued. "I remember that he didn't want any part of a Confederate uniform. It's odd to see him in such dress."

"He had the right intention," said Jay. "He preferred love over war. Unfortunately, he lacked conviction, and was coerced into wearing a rebel uniform. But either way, death would have come. Had he not worn that uniform, he'd been

108

taken out by Confederate bounty hunters.   Actually, he doesn't know it, but he's on training wheels."

"So, what's next?" asked Lucy.

"Leonard and I are going in after him," replied Jay.

"We're what?" bellowed Leonard. "That's necromancy. I don't want to be any part of that."

"Leonard, it's not like we're raising zombies or dead bodies."

"Okay. What then is this?"

"Look at it this way, Leonard. It is possible to divide one soul into many parts. You recognized the man's soul, not his appearance. His soul was not apparent in what he wore or how he looked any more than the color of his wife's skin. You recognized a part of yourself, a part of your soul that slipped away decades ago. Take courage and reclaim it, Leonard. Let the man wearing a deliberate Confederate disguise merge back into you. Reclaim yourself, and you'll recognize Lucy for who she is!"

Without a second thought, Leonard jumped feet first into the well. Jay turned to Lucy. "Meet us at the foot of the sink hole!"

Lucy, followed by Herk and Baba, walked quickly to the sink hole. Upon arriving, the two men stood at the entrance of the sink hole, soaking wet. Leonard and Lucy embraced, bringing them closer to joy, a place where they'd once been.

CHAPTER 36

OVERCOMERS

ucy looked over at Leonard and casually asked, "We haven't seen Jay in several days. I wonder why?"

"Maybe he's giving us time to sort through these experiences," replied Leonard. "Jay can guide us through places we've never been, but we have to process them. No one can do that for us."

"Tell me, Leonard, how do you feel taking on a soul fragment?"

"It's like being given a transfusion where there is a heightened shift in consciousness. It's like gaining a bouquet of AP points."

"Bouquet of AP points?" Lucy chuckled.

"Yeah, a bouquet of awareness points. It's like looking through an improved lens. Everything is magnified -- the colors, the sounds, my memory. I recall things I've never experienced in this lifetime. I feel like I've known you in past lifetimes. Tom's love for the blind girl is what I recognized when I came out of that sink hole and fell into your embrace. I experienced you as a beautiful bouquet of white roses -- in touch, in feel, and in taste -- magnified a thousand-fold, an experience even better than sex. What if there is a soul and, somehow, mine slipped away?"

Lucy walked over to Leonard and hugged his neck. "Thank you." She affectionately looked him in the eye and continued. "Really, better that sex? Do you think that we can successfully enter into and maintain that kind of relationship?"

"I hope so; I'll not pass it up. The man in the well was like looking at myself in a mirror. We were both in a swamp or a dark wood or on a high sea without a compass or rudder. I lost my vocabulary in a quagmire that I could not talk my way out of. While stumbling in the dark, I found the light; I reached out and took hold of a bouquet of gleaming white roses. I watched as they melted down to one single white rose. I recognized our reunion."

"I recognized you the day we met," said Lucy, "wandering around that exposition. Do you remember what you said to me?"

"Of course. You were reading Nietzsche. I asked if you read Nietzsche because you felt misunderstood or because you seek the position of an overcomer. Do you remember your reply?"

"Certainly, I do: 'You are just the person I'm fated to meet.'" Lucy paused and looked questioningly at Leonard. "Do you know why?"

"No, tell me."

"I was reading the story of Zarathustra, a prophet much like Jesus. Jesus came preaching dying of the self; Zarathustra came preaching overcoming the self. I didn't see the terms as contradictory. We have to embrace dying in order to overcome the self. Memory is never erased in an immortal soul; we learn from memory, overcome the hardships, and heal. Forgiveness is an overcoming that doesn't come easy. Nietzsche said that we killed God. No, God is not dead. Man has relegated God to a place of forgetfulness, like that quagmire that you could not walk out

111

of. In our age, humans affirm only one side of Jay's coin, the material world. Man's reach is no further than his grasp. One has to reach beyond his grasp, like you did to overcome the swamp. Don't ask me how I knew, but I knew that you were the one seeking to reach beyond your grasp, and that is precisely what I'd been looking for."

"I've read lines from Browning that are etched in my memory. 'Ah, but a man's reach should exceed his grasp, or what's a heaven for?'" Leonard paused. "Now, given the opportunity, I find myself reaching for something that I feel is within my grasp, to take a look at the past where, I believe, we've lived before, in the Middle Ages. I'm drawn to it."

"We've been there, Leonard. I'm sure of it."

"What does it mean to learn or benefit from that time?" questioned Leonard.

"Why don't we find out."

CHAPTER 37

Making ready for soul food

A voice cried out, "Wait up, guys!"

Lucy and Leonard turned around to see Jay hurrying toward them.

"Jay, where have you been? Good to see you," sounded Lucy.

Jay responded, "I showed up at the Airstream a bit early. I assume you are staying in the cabin this evening."

"Yeah, the interior is finished, and we've got furniture in place. We can roll away the bed and the kitchen counter. We're ready to ease into this unique dwelling place," said Lucy.

Leonard grimaced as he looked Jay over from head to toe. "Jay, what's with the tan? You look four shades darker."

"And what's with the business suit? You look like a politician," remarked Lucy. "I've never known you to dress up like that."

"Oh, the dress and skin color. They're deliberate disguises. I didn't have time to change and wanted to hurry back before you guys spent too much time in dreamland."

"Deliberate disguises for what?" asked Lucy.

"I've been doing some multidimensional work with the herd soul."

"The herd soul?" questioned Leonard.

"Yeah, I'm on the national scene advising and guiding herd souls."

"Are you having fun?" asked Leonard.

"No! I'm working with tribal minds, souls from the Civil War, now living in the 21st century. Many of these souls think evidence-based science is fake. Despite the death count, they won't get vaccinated. I like working with you both, especially when I'm hungry."

Upon entering the cabin, Jay looked around. "Yes! This looks great!" Noticing that the kitchen countertop had been placed over the well, and that the bed had been moved to the side of the room, Jay continued, "I commend you both on using some common sense. You can't sleep over a prevailing source of power every night. Where I've recently been working, folks want to sleep over power and beg to be sucked under by it. Those knuckleheads would sleep and fuck on that bed every night. They'd desecrate this sacred place. We'd really have a serious plumbing problem living right over a shit hole of lost souls."

"The experiences that we channeled were so transforming that we decided not to make sleeping over a power source into a routine," said Leonard.

"Yes, anyone who channels over this well needs debriefing." Jay paused, "As I've explained, debriefing sounds military, like a hidden agenda or remote viewing for an advantage. You folks carry on channeling without any hidden agenda. You both channeled for information, and you came back and used that information to regain Leonard's soul fragment. Now, that sounds simple, but it could have been much more complicated had you not attempted to rescue the right soul."

Jay moved to the countertop positioned over the well and remarked, "Great place for a kitchen! You're talking about real soul food prepared in this area – purified by harmonic tones, Lucy. This will help to soften the strain on your kidney."

"Thanks, Jay," replied Lucy. "I'll certainly not forget that. I, too, believe in the sanctity of the home. This is our new home. It's only one room, but its atmosphere is creative. It is a place where children can be raised and transformation can take place every day."

"Yes," replied Leonard. "The image of a home is an image of something to care for, maintain, and keep alive. This thought prehends our action."

"You've got it, Leonard!" said Jay. "Don't kill that image!"

"Now," said Lucy, "it's time for some of that good soul food."

CHAPTER 38

Divine illumination: trust in VALIS

Jay asked, "Do you guys really think that you're ready to go back 1500 years into someone else's skin. Most likely, you're not going to recognize the old you in body or in mind. Recognition does not come all at once, neither does inner vision. The process takes time."

"What?" replied Lucy. "You mean emerge into that person's experience, that person's inner world comprising the emotional and psychological part that we can only guess at?"

"You'll both have to take the next trip down to a whole new level. Your recent channeling trips were more in line with sitting back looking at a movie where the subject was always at a distance. The full benefit of learning to live in VALIS is to crawl into that person's skin. You'll not be remotely viewing anything; this will be a serious entry into lives of those who have lived before. Therein lies long lost memories that need to be reprocessed upon return."

"First, I think we need to know something about who we're dealing with," said Leonard. "We need to know who you are, why you're here, and why the deliberate disguise."

"Telling you the answer is one thing, but showing is quite another. That's why the backward look, to have a clear recognition and take it forward into your lived experience. With that, your psychic alignment will resonate a frequency approximating VALIS."

"Sounds cultic to me," said Lucy.

"And that it may be, Lucy, and it will come down to your choice to love it or leave it." Jay turned to Leonard. "Now, to answer your first question, 'who am I?' I was created in the twentieth-first dimension by the VAST ACTIVE LIVING INTELLIGENT SOUL. I am a microscopic imperfect copy of an infinite soul. I was created with the capacity to travel through all dimensions less than the 21st, including those dimensions with numbers less than one. Some have called me Hermes; others have labeled me Christ or the Buddha. Some have labeled me Satan himself. I would more aptly be described as a guide of souls, a thought adjuster, a psychopomp, or an angel. That is, straight up, who I am and where I come from with no disguise or deception."

"Now, to answer the second question, 'why am I here?' My job as a guide of souls is to take you across boundaries that you would otherwise be unable to cross. In so doing, you learn and grow. At some point, the training wheels come off, and I leave. With your own rudder, compass, and sail you begin to navigate your own course through multi-dimensions of time and space."

"So, what's with the disguise and the mask?" asked Leonard.

"That's the very reason I came into the third dimension, to find those who would not be offended by me. I found you both; you accepted a person branded a schizophrenic, a person others shunned and wanted to put away. We became friends, and here I am, just Jay. 'I am who I am'."

"Well," said Leonard, "there's been no hick-up so far; you've got me out of a rut, and now I'm making music with a remarkable young woman. I never anticipated anything like this."

"Grace comes unexpectedly, like a thief in the night, Leonard."

"There's no reason not to trust you, Jay," said Lucy, "but how far does our story play out before we're confronted with your boss, this VALIS character. Maybe the "S" in VALIS stands for a system and not a soul. Who's to say we're not dealing with some kind of *Wizard of Oz* – a phony behind a system that imprisons other souls?"

"Lucy, I can tell you this; the writers of the Old Testament used the acronym, YHWH, to stand for God. His magnitude and power are so great that the Israelites were not allowed to even speak or pronounce his name. YHWH is who he or she is. The anachronym, VALIS, is a Christian reimagining of YHWH with a twist, the Incarnation. God, himself, is a VAST-ACTIVE-LIVING-INTELLIGENT-SOUL which is greater than anything we can think of or imagine. In short, we can't even imagine what we don't know about this self-organizing dynamic power. Buddhists say that what we witness and observe is only a dependent arising."

"To put it in a nutshell," said Lucy, "we have to walk out in faith over an abyss."

"That's putting it mildly," said Jay. "I'm talking about what you will encounter: blood, guts, murder and betrayal. This will not be a straight walk in the park; learning to overcome suffering and death never is."

Lucy and Jay turned to one another in silence.

Jay continued, "I'd say your imagination carries your grasp beyond your reach. Faith closes the gap; it comes as a part of the living package. Channeling back in time and acquiring long lost memories and experiences may be your tickets to Divine Illumination where trust in VALIS is not a problem. Trust may take you both to a place of many mansions where the experience of divine forgiveness reigns in your heart and mind.   If you internalize the reality of forgiveness and practice it, you will take on the mind of God, which is Divine Illumination. You will reflect this presence, and death will not make you stumble."

CHAPTER 39

Reliving the Past

Lucy looked directly at Leonard and spoke up. "Oh, it was horrible, terrifying!" She pulled herself up and moved her legs over the side of the bed. "Did you see what happened?"

"Yes, I saw every bit of it."

"What a way to go, I was filled with terror," said Lucy, shivering as she spoke.

"Yeah, it was quick. Tell me what happened."

"I woke up, like it was just a dream. And now, here I am, over fifteen hundred years later in a safe place, alive and kicking. They killed me and other people for sport, Leonard. I was in a lady's skin. I harbored her memories and her fears, and cried her tears." Lucy paused, then quickly turned to Leonard. "I shit and pissed on myself, not knowing the real me. We need to consider the unintended consequences of merging into another living being. What about you, Leonard, did an unknown someone kill you for sport?"

"No. I was living in the experience of a man named Alypius. At the time, he didn't expect to become a part of the mob, but did. The character became a moral weakling, and he knew it. No, no one killed me for sport. I was in Carthage studying law at the time. My friend, Aurelius, later known as St. Augustine, was a teacher of rhetoric who came up from our hometown to gather students. It was fortuitous that we reunited because we shared the same pressing need which was to seek wisdom and live a virtuous life. One day, several of my classmates came into my room drinking, saying that the stadium was open, and I should go with them to the gladiatorial event currently taking place. They knew my piety, laughed at it, and persisted in pushing me to accompany them. One of them said, 'Alypius, your virtue is frail. A virtuous man, with the strength of his convictions, would not be overcome by the sight of death.' In the moment, I did not want to appear weak to my friends. I could not resist going with them, yet, my resistance was such that they had to drag me into the stadium. I took a seat and closed my eyes, determined not to look. Time after time, in a repetitive rhythm, the crowd would cheer and rise to their feet. On occasion, a victorious combatant would pause and look to the crowd for a decision. A thumbs down meant death; a thumbs up meant mercy."

"At the end of the event, one soul stood motionless in the center of the arena. It was you, Lucy, a blind young woman. She could have been a goddess symbolizing justice. The combatant paused. The crowd stood up, and I stood with them; this time I opened my eyes. The thumbs were all down and the combatant, once again, hesitated, stepped back, and spat on the ground giving a middle finger to the crowd. Then, turning, he took her head with one blow of his sword. Was it mercy that dropped to the ground that day, or did justice also take a fall? I didn't know that death would take so many. Again and again, I would return to the stadium with my friends, participating in these murderous events. I was not appalled by the sight of death; I was addicted to it. "

"Leonard, how did it feel to be in the skin of Alypius? What happens when we continue to channel others in the flesh and live through the smell and feel of death? Do we become addicted, too?"

"I lived on for a while, haunted by what I took in," replied Leonard. "I was experiencing a real case of PTSD. Augustine was not just a teacher; he was like a big brother. When he became a teacher, I learned rhetoric from him. One day Augustine was struggling with his unruly passions and worldly ambitions. We were in a garden, under a tree, when he got up and walked away. He returned, saying that he'd heard children at play singing: 'pick up and read, pick up and read.' He thought it odd because he could not identify where the voices were coming from or why such a verse would be sung by children. Augustine thought this experience might be God speaking to him. He randomly opened the Bible to Paul's letter to the Romans and read from it: 'not in carousing and drunkenness, not in sexual excess and lust, not quarreling and jealousy.' My troubles were his, and God's Word spoke to both of us. I felt a softening of my heart and knew that it was time to let go of my addiction to violence. Augustine had to overcome the flesh with all of his passions, and so did I."

"So, Alypius, you lived and made a transformation, but I died a brutal death by the sword. You never lived in terror," remarked Lucy with a chuckle. "Think about it, Leonard. So, I go out in terror, and you hang around and live. I guess you're ready to do this again. How about we rent *Spartacus* and kick back with popcorn."

Leonard took Lucy's hand and squeezed it. "Lucy," he asked, "are you ready for a change in scenery?"

"Oh, yes, most definitely!"

"Let's take Herk and Baba in the side-car down the Henry Horton Highway and see where it takes us."

"Leonard, let's roll this damn bed back where it belongs."

CHAPTER 40

Soul twins

Leonard fired up the motorcycle and hopped on. Lucy took the seat behind him and looked over at Herk and Baba. "You boys get in." They jumped up into the sidecar. Leonard pulled out of the driveway and bolted off toward the Horton Highway. They cruised around the Henry Horton State Park and headed toward Columbia. About five miles down the road, Leonard spotted a sign that read, Duck River Canoe Rentals, and turned off the road. They came to a small campground where a few cars were parked. They noticed several make-shift outhouses beside a path leading to the river. As they made their way to the nearby path, Lucy noticed a car with Florida plates. "How does someone from Florida find a place like this?" she casually mused.

The two pets followed the couple to the shore of the river. They watched as a young couple took their place in a canoe and paddled out of sight. Looking down the river bank, they saw a woman sitting with her head turned away from them sipping from a bottle of Jack Daniels.

"She looks like she's in distress, Leonard."

"Yeah, maybe you should check on her."

They watched in surprise as Herk ran to the woman, wagging his tail and licking her face, and Baba jumped into her lap.

"Oh, my goodness," snapped Lucy, springing to her feet darting toward the woman. "Herk, Baba, get off that lady."

The woman turned toward Lucy and, suddenly, took on a look of surprise. "Lucy, is that you?"

"Cana, Cana Sherwood, I can't believe it!"

Wiping her tears away, Cana stood up and the two embraced.

Lucy turned to Leonard. "Leonard, this is the friend I told you about." She turned back to Cana, "Meet my fiancée, Leonard."

"Nice to meet you, Leonard. I would shake your hands but mine are wet with tears."

"Cana, my dear, I thought you were in Orlando. Why are you here, in Tennessee – on the Duck River?" asked Lucy.

"Hank Sherwood left me for another woman."

"What? You just got married three years ago."

Cana burst out in tears. Lucy embraced her and patted her back. "It's going to be all right."

Cana managed to pull herself together. "It's ironic. Here I am drinking whisky and wanting to walk off into that river. This is the place where Hank wrote a hit song and sang it in the Blue Bird Cafe. He's the one who ought to be out here with an aching heart wanting to drink himself into that river."

"Come on, Cana, come with us," said Lucy, "We don't live far from here. You don't need to be out here all alone."

"Thank you so much, Lucy."

Lucy looked over at Leonard and pointed to the overturned bottle of Jack Daniels. As they moved out of the river area toward the parking lot, Leonard dropped the bottle in a trash barrel. Upon reaching the parking area, Lucy saw the car with the Florida plates.

"I'll drive you to our place. Leonard can follow us back on his new bike. You can tell me how all this happened on the way."

Noticing the motorcycle, Cana walked over to it and touched it. "A motorcycle with a side-car. I can't believe that you showed up just when I needed a miracle."

Falling to her feet, Cana lifted her hands toward the sky and shouted, "Thank you, Jesus!"

Lucy and Leonard looked at each other as if to say, "What?"

Herk jumped in the car with Cana and Lucy. They both watched through the windshield as Baba hopped in the side-car beside Leonard. "That's not supposed to happen," said Cana. Do your dog and cat always ride together?"

"Oh that," remarked Lucy. "The cat's taken to Leonard; Baba sleeps near Leonard's side of the bed, and Herk sleeps beside me."

"My God," Lucy," said Cana, "that's a sign! Those pets are soul twins. You guys are like the pets; you guys are soul twins."

CHAPTER 41

THE TENNESSEE GHOST RIDER

Cana's car, followed by the motorcycle, pulled into the driveway. Lucy cut off the engine and turned her attention to Herk in the back seat. Herk stood up on all fours with a book hanging out of his mouth. His head dangled over the front seat.

"Give me the book, Herk," said Lucy. The dog dropped the book as Cana's hand reached out and grabbed it. The girls face's met. "No need to apologize for Herk. It's another sign," said Cana. She held up the book. "This Scofield is my strength and comfort!"

When Cana stepped into the Airstream, she carried her Scofield with her in a leather tote case. "Hey, you girls make yourself comfortable; I'll make a fresh pot of coffee," said Leonard, moving into the kitchen area.

The girls took a seat and Lucy, leaning over, asked, "Cana, are you alright?"

"Lucy, my dear, I was drunk, but now I'm sober," replied Cana, as she broke into a gleaming smile. "My tears have been washed away."

"Okay, that's great," said Lucy, sitting back in her seat.

Leonard entered the living area and took a seat beside Lucy. "You seem pretty clear-headed to me, Cana. I'm glad you're not floating face down in the Duck River."

"I prayed for guidance, and God led me to this moment."

Lucy and Leonard looked at one another, as if to say, "What?"

Cana lifted up her leather tote case. "It's all in here," said Cana. *"For by grace are ye saved through faith; and that not of yourselves: it is the gift of God."*

"We're all ears, Cana. We're here for you."

"Yes," said Leonard. "Talking is good -- it's therapeutic?"

"In my case, confession is the word." Cana paused, Lucy and Leonard waited for her to continue. "I didn't listen to God and married the wrong man."

"I was there at your wedding, Cana. You both seemed very happy, cemented together, a tight bond."

"But the bond wasn't with superglue, Lucy. After the wedding, something didn't feel right, and I could not put my finger on it. I remembered your advice, Lucy: 'When in trouble look to the Lord'."

"I prayed for guidance, and it all came together when we walked into the parking lot, and I spotted Leonard's motorcycle with the side-car. In an instant, my soul turned, and I was born again."

"Okay," said Lucy, "what are you talking about?"

"Yes," echoed Leonard, "what's this about my motorcycle?"

"Have either of you experienced an instant change?"

"I'm not entirely sure what you mean by an 'instant change,'" replied Lucy.

"Are you talking about transformation?" asked Leonard.

"Something like that," replied Cana, "but it's more about the bond to Hank; the bond breaks and so does my heart. I find myself on the riverside with a bottle of Jack Daniels. When the pieces come together, when I see the hand of God at work, that he has led me to this moment, my thoughts and emotions were no longer the same. Now I am free to forgive Hank and live again. It's a change of heart."

"I sincerely hope that this works for you, Cana, and is not merely a defense against your loss," said Lucy. "Forgiveness can slip away when you're lonely."

"I have assurance, Lucy, and I will remember this day and the moment of my receiving His spirit, forever. I prayed for guidance, and we moved to Nashville. I prayed that Hank would write a successful country song. We came to Chapel Hill looking for material; it was at the Duck River that Hank wrote *The Tennessee Ghost Rider.* That you folks showed up when you did was no coincidence. But it all came together in a transforming moment when I spotted Leonard's motorcycle and side-car. The Ghost Rider – the one in Hank's song -- prowls Tennessee in a side-car motorcycle."

Leonard and Lucy turned to one another with a look of wonder. They said nothing and turned back to Cana.

"I haven't heard the song," said Lucy.

Leonard shook his head. "I haven't either."

"Hank's singing next Friday night at The Wild Mule Saloon on Printer's Alley. I'm sure he'll sing that song several times."

CHAPTER 42

TRUST IN THE LORD

ucy and Leonard stepped out of the Airstream. It was beginning to drizzle and was almost dark. "It's chilly out here," said Lucy pulling her arms to her body.

"Yes, I need to get back to the cabin," said Leonard, "before it pours. Are you sure you're going to be safe tomorrow?"

"I think so. I've not known Hank to be violent," assured Lucy. "I'll call Hank and ask if I can pick up Cana's things and feel out his reaction. I'll see what happens."

"Love you, dear," said Leonard as he kissed Lucy on the cheek and quickly moved down the wooded path to their rustic home.

"I love you, too," cried Lucy, watching Leonard vanish in the dark.

Lucy stepped back into the Airstream; she walked down the hall to the back end of the home where she found Cana fast asleep. Lucy covered her with the blanket and returned to the front room. She noticed Cana's tote case on a shelf; the one that contained her Scofield Bible. Next to the case were three books which she and Leonard had recently picked up from the Franklin library: *The Confessions of St.*

Augustine, The Consolation of Philosophy, and the Love Story of Abelard and Heloise. Lucy took a seat and began reading *The Confessions.*

Lucy woke up the following morning with the book in her hand. She heard Cana in the kitchen and smelled the fresh coffee; Cana brought Lucy the cup of coffee and set it on the side table. "Go freshen up and I'll have breakfast ready in a jiff." Lucy took several sips of the brew, then left to take a shower.

When Lucy returned, breakfast was on the table. She was dressed and ready for the day, her short sandy hair combed back. "Oh, don't you look nice," said Cana. "Here sit down and enjoy the breakfast."

Lucy sat down at the table and looked thoughtfully at her friend. "Cana, you're a good friend. Who would remember the eggs over light and the steel cut oats? You remembered."

"And I remember how our friendship began," said Cana. "It was fun skipping out of chapel on Fridays and smoking grass in the park. That didn't set well with Father George when he was teaching us catechism."

"I enjoyed gassing up the old priest," added Lucy, "asking stupid questions that he couldn't possibly answer."

"The only thing I got out of Christian School was music," added Cana.

"Me too. Hey, do you still play the flute?"

"Sure do," replied Cana. "It's a part of my stuff – stuff that I need to go get."

Lucy insisted that she could go over to Hank's place and pick up Cana's belongings. "You don't have to come."

Cana changed the subject and said, "I noticed you were reading *The Confessions.* We read that book in our senior year. What was the Sister's name?"

"Sister…Sister Garthwaite!" exclaimed Lucy.

"Yes, that's it! Sister Garthwaite. Boy was she a butterball!"

"Yes!" laughed Lucy, "Watch your diet or you'll get... Garthweight." Cana and Lucy were hysterical with laughter. Cana composed herself.

"I'm going to be serious," said Cana. "*The Confessions* was a serious book, but none of us could understand it. I can hear the Sister now: 'The hand of God moves and where it stops nobody knows. Confess your sins and trust in the Lord.'"

"Yes, that's it! 'Where it stops, trust in the Lord.'"

"Don't make me laugh," said Cana, straining to hold back another outburst. "This is serious, I promise you, Lucy. This Saint 'fessed up to more mistakes than we could count. I 'fessed up to one, and only one mistake, that I followed the wrong hand. I followed my hand and married the wrong man."

Lucy burst out laughing again. "You made one mistake. For fifteen years the Saint shacked up with one woman and dumped her. Then he took in another and dumped her. He confessed these wrong turns, but I don't remember him ever calling these women by name."

"That's not me, Lucy. I've got to go back and face the music, look Hank straight in the eye, and say: 'I forgive you' and mean it from the bottom of my heart. Then I will walk out with my stuff, holding my head high and never look back with bitterness or regret. When my mended heart connects with my flesh, I'll know that I have trusted in the Lord."

"Let's go and get your stuff, Cana. Leonard and I are moving to the cabin, and you can stay here for a while."

CHAPTER 43

Wₑᵢᵣ𝒹

Weird

Lucy filled the side-car with groceries, books, and a laptop. She fired up the motorcycle and headed back to the cabin. Herk and Baba jumped down off the deck to greet her. Leonard emerged from the cabin and helped to bring the things in. He set the items down on an earth-tone coffee table they had recently bought, and asked, "How did things go today?"

"What do you want to hear first: the good news or the interesting stuff?"

"Hit me with the good stuff first."

"We had no problem," said Lucy, plopping down in a recliner. "Cana retrieved the few things she had and told Hank what she had to say, and, thank God, he didn't make a fuss. We were out of there."

"So, Hank was home?" asked Leonard.

"Not at first," said Lucy. "Hank and Cana had rented a small cottage near the Meharry Medical College. Hank wasn't there when we arrived; Cana had a key, and we went in. About five minutes later, Hank walked in with a strange-looking young girl covered with tattoos, had black nail polish and orange hair. Hank went into the bedroom to talk with

Cana asking the girl for some privacy. The girl and I talked a bit in the living room. She told me she worked making prosthetics and had taken off for the day to be with Hank. She seemed uneasy and suddenly blurted out, 'who did you come here to fuck, Hank? I'm waiting.' He came right out; they went into another smaller bedroom and closed the door. Hank had some weird stuff in that extra bedroom; I caught a glimpse of pictures he had hanging on the wall: Nathan Bedford Forrest and ghost riders carrying torches. On the back of the door was a poster of Adolf Hitler doing a *zieg heil*."

"No shit," Leonard shook his head and smiled. "Tattoos, black fingernails, orange hair, prosthetics, ghost riders, Nathan Bedford Forrest and Adolf Hitler. It doesn't get any weirder than that."

"On the way home," said Lucy, "Cana filled in the blanks. When they came to Nashville, Hank got into Civil War history. After that, they drove to Chapel Hill, the birth place of Nathan Bedford Forrest. Hank came back to Nashville and wrote *The Tennessee Ghost Rider*.

"Did Cana tell you that the song made Number One on Billboard?" asked Leonard.

"Yes, and the country crowd is going ape over it."

"And a crowd is also fighting like hell to keep the bust of Forrest in the State Capital."

"It sounds like the Civil War is still going on," replied Lucy, "extending from our State Capital to the Insurrection on the grounds of the United States Capitol. These Confederates even have a shaman who is as weird as Hank's little prosthetic-making friend, all mixed in with MAGA folks and paramilitary types."

"I can't imagine a major recording studio taking on a song about Forrest."

"It's not about Forrest, Leonard. It's about an unidentified ghost rider in search of a mystery in Tennessee. People can read anything they want listening to the lyrics, even tease out Mickey Mouse. Hank met Mickey Gentry, a retired country music legend. When Gentry heard the song, he begged Hank to let him sing the song and produce it. Rebel Radio played the song, and the thing took off. Mickey Gentry is making a comeback."

Lucy got out her laptop and fired it up. "I want you to look at this," she said, typing in a name. Leonard took a knee at her side and looked at the screen. A picture appeared showing Field Marshal Erwin Rommel in a Nazi uniform, fully decorated with an Iron Cross pinned on his collar. Lucy slowly scrolled through the pages. "These are sightings of Rommel riding through Tennessee and Mississippi on a side-car motorcycle, even going up into East Tennessee. There is a section in this article that I remote viewed, here and in Clifton." Lucy pointed directly at that part of the article.

"Damn, it is there!" said Leonard. "The very thing you channeled."

"It gets better, Leonard." Lucy scrolled to the next page and pointed to a picture. "The man on the left is Manfred Rommel, the mayor of Stuttgart, Germany. He's Rommel's son. He assured the American historian on the right that his father was never in Tennessee or Mississippi. Rommel is the Tennessee Ghost Rider on a side-car motorcycle."

"And that's exactly what Jay told us." said Leonard. "Rommel was remote viewing from somewhere in Germany, and you had channeled his appearance from our place and from Clifton. He was never in either place."

"Well, that's our spin on it, Leonard. Our take is less real than orange hair and weirder to boot."

"We all seemed to be swayed by what appears to be fiction," replied Leonard, "but the culture of this place and the people who live here continue to live out of the past. Moral change is slow to come, and that's where my last channeling took me with my friend, Augustine. He taught me a lesson on the misuse of words. Being a teacher of how words are used, he had a keen ability to discern lies based on the biases of a crowd or a group of people. For St. Augustine, the world was a text, and most read it to serve their own interest. His insight gave me a wisdom into the moral depravity of a clan, a tribe, or a social network. Such insight provides conviction, and it took conviction to resist a crowd of peers when I followed them to the stadium to watch your brutal murder."

CHAPTER 44

Escape Fiction

It seemed as if Leonard wanted to go back in. Addressing Lucy, he said, "I realize that you got 'the bejesus' scared out of you the last trip in, but now's not the time to run away. You learn by facing your fears. The crowd fears death; they run away from it. We're not the crowd, Lucy!"

"Leonard, come on," said Lucy. "I'm not putting my head on the chopping block again."

"Look, Lucy, the crowd is dead, VALIS lives! You're the girl with the Christian upbringing; what about the Incarnation? Don't you want to get a handle on what that's all about?"

"What are you getting at, Leonard?"

"We live in a world of flux and always have; it's always on the move. It's moving so fast that politics is stupid piled on top of stupid. It's all escape fiction anyway you choose to look at it. Now, do you want to buy into the mind of QAnon? Hey, those guys are alive and kicking. MAGA morons will do anything to stay alive and take control; they want to follow a leader and buy into stupid; they come out being used and often going to jail. We need to get on the right side of escape fiction. I mean really learn to face what the crowd runs from –

death. We need to run toward death and somehow learn to live. If God or VALIS made us in His image, I don't see Trump or any of his MAGA crowd as trusty, suffering servants."

"Look Leonard," said Lucy, "if you want to go back in and give up your head in a living retake, be my guest. The only escape fiction I want any part of is you and twelve notes. We make music together and carry twelve notes everywhere."

"That's my point, Lucy! But the crowd is as slippery as an icy slope. Most crowds are out of control; they have a hive mind. They are the ones who excommunicate you from your own mind and the mind of God! On my last trip in, Augustine told me a story. The pagans brought Augustine to the point of conversion. After that, he took on a new mind. The story was about a hotel that all sorts of travelers would visit going in and out of Athens. All of these travelers used the same bed. The proprietor would come in as they lay sleeping and force their bodies to fit the bed. If the legs were too long, he would cut them off; if their bodies were too short, he would stretch them to fit. These travelers woke up the next day and went on their way, not noticing what had happened to them. Week after week, year after year, they kept returning to this hotel until finally, they could not recognize themselves. They were conformed to the side-show of their time, in Athens. My friend was not conformed to this world. He took the pagan notion of the Good, which was the highest platonic form, and made it living and personal. He became a saint!"

"Leonard, are you telling me that you're going back in?"

"Yes, I am, Lucy! I'm going back in!"

"But why, why are you doing this?"

"When I first met you, I had reached the end of my vocabulary, the sum total of all that I have ever experienced in this life. I was at a dead end, going nowhere. The dread is not being able to die and move on in a different mind. We have the opportunity to move beyond the herd mind, to reach beyond our grasp. I mean reach for God and attain the assurance that we are authentically situated in His mind."

"Isn't assurance already here, Leonard? Do you want to be born again?"

"Born again is different for each of us. I see where Cana is coming from, Lucy. But, in a changing world, I have to keep the images alive and on the move. I want to observe the past in silent attendance and move on without the fear of death. I want to discern the coming kingdom."

"Since you're so hell bent on going back in, would you mind if I pick the time and place, and the person whose skin you will be slipping into?"

"Will you be coming in with me, Lucy."

"You bet, Leonard. I'll be right there to hold your hand. No backing out, Leonard."

"Lucy, you have that look as if you're holding back on something."

"You want to face death, Leonard? Then practice what you preach! Get on the right side of escape fiction; let the crowd take your head!"

CHAPTER 45

FIRST DATE AFTER THE STORM

Cana heard a knock on the front door of the Airstream. "Lucy... Leonard, is that you?" she exclaimed, as she quickly moved to the door. She cracked the door open and looked out at a man in a brown corduroy jacket wearing sunglasses.

Looking through the screen door, Jeff remarked, "You're not Lucy."

"No, I'm Cana, Lucy's friend."

"I'm Jeff, Leonard's friend."

"Oh, you're the friend that sold Leonard this property; what a pleasant surprise. Please come in; Lucy and Leonard will be here shortly. We're headed to the Wild Mule Saloon. Leonard wants to see my ex sing and play...an original. Make yourself at home, Jeff, while I finish getting ready." Blithefully, Cana stripped down to her bikini underwear and bra.

"I don't mean to interrupt...," said Jeff looking away. "I just dropped by to say hello. I didn't know they had a guest."

"I'm not a guest; Lucy and Leonard are letting me stay here."

Cana reached for her jeans and slipped them on. Jeff turned back to check out the tight fit. Cana took up a silk long

139

sleeve cowgirl shirt, put it on, and tucked it in. "Jeff, you're not interrupting a thing. In fact, you're just in time to be my date."

"Oh, I am?"

"Okay, great," said Cana. "You'll fit in fine, a tourist taking in the sights." Jeff watched as Cana sat down, put on cowboy boots, stood up, turned around, and asked, "How do I look, Jeff?"

"Splendid, you look splendid."

Cana sat down across from Jeff. She bent over so that her head rested in the palms of her hands; her auburn hair fell around her cheeks. "Tell me about yourself, Jeff."

"I know that the last time I went to see my ex, I wound up in the hospital."

"Last time I saw my ex, he was glad to be rid of me. So, neither of us have a thing to worry about. My ex and I are no longer friends."

Jeff paused to collect his thoughts. "I don't know that I'm up to this." He shook his head and Cana looked on attentively. "This is my first date since the break-up. I'm being frank; my confidence isn't there yet."

Cana reached over and took Jeff's hands. Their heads met. "This is also my first date and, win or lose, I'm up for it." Cana got quiet and slowly removed Jeff's shades, licked her finger and rubbed it across Jeff's lips. Jeff sat there goggle-eyed. "Jeff, you're not a shoddy knockoff of the man who dumped me; it's no coincidence that you showed up. Just pretend that I'm the original and your ex is the shoddy knockoff. This is a first date after the storm for both of us. Jeff, I have your back; cover mine. Believe that I love you, and you'll do the same for me. We'll see what happens."

"Okay, Cana, it sounds like a plan."

"Hey, guys, we're here." Lucy and Leonard were standing at the screen door wearing cowboy hats and blue jeans.

"Jeff, old buddy," said Leonard with a note of surprise, "You're just in time! We're headed to Nashville!"

CHAPTER 46

THE LAST OUTFIT

Lucy and Leonard sat in the front seat of Lucy's car, and Lucy drove. Jeff and Cana sat in the back seat. "I hope you're up to this, Cana," said Lucy, looking back over the seat.

Cana, moved over to Jeff and took hold of his arm. "I think I have ample backup, Lucy."

"I've never been in the Wild Mule Saloon or on Music Row, much less met a country singer," said Leonard. "Cana's ex sounds like a jerk; I like to meet jerks – I look for the object lesson!"

"Cana mentioned something about an original song. What's that all about?" asked Jeff.

"He's written a hit song, and it's gone to his head, Jeff," replied Cana.

"What's it about?"

"You'll hear it tonight."

"I've never heard it either," interjected Leonard. "The girls tell me that it's about a ghost that rides around on a side-car motorcycle."

"Hey, Leonard, maybe you're the ghost!" exclaimed Jeff. "You're the only guy around who has one."

Speaking directly to Jeff, Cana grinned. "It's all very strange, trust me."

Directing his attention to Lucy, Jeff asked. "Can I trust your friend?"

"Jeff, she's the most trustworthy person you will ever meet." Lucy hesitated and then added, "But she's liable to jerk your chain."

"She's succeeded at that, right off the bat."

"Well," said Cana, "I always have a good reason for jerking a chain -- a reaction sends a message."

"Cana, have you been a naughty girl?" joked Lucy.

Jeff laughed. "Hell yes, she's been naughty. Your chain- jerking friend stripped down and dressed in front of me, a complete stranger."

"Jeff," said Cana sympathetically, "you needed an imaginative message, something to break you out those sun shades and that brown corduroy jacket. I want a look, even a glance, at the real you."

"You're one to talk," said Jeff. "You're a cowgirl tonight; what about the real you?"

"You haven' seen through my last outfit, Jeff."

"Seen through your last outfit?" echoed Jeff.

"Yeah, my bra and panties." Laughter filled the car as they pulled into Garage Parking.

CHAPTER 47

Dedication at the Wild Mule Saloon

The sun was setting as the foursome entered the Wild Mule Saloon. A large man, looking like a cross between a wild horse and a mule, approached them. "I'm sorry folks, but we're filled up tonight; social distancing makes reservations a must."

"I'm Cana Sherwood, Hank Sherwood's wife." She acknowledged Lucy and Leonard. "These are our friends."

"All right, Mrs. Sherwood and friends, follow me."

The group took front seats near the stage, sat down, then ordered a pitcher of beer. The scattered crowd began to gather as the band tuned up. Suddenly, a voice sounded from the stage. "All right, are you ready boys? One, two, three," and the upbeat rhythm and lyrics flowing from the band filled the room. Jeff rose from his seat, took off his jacket and led Cana to the dance floor. Others followed, as Lucy and Leonard watched from their table. "I think she has jerked something loose in him," said Leonard trying to speak over the music. "That's how I remember him in our college days." Lucy gave Leonard a thumbs-up. The music softened with a ballad, and Cana and Jeff found themselves in an embrace.

The music stopped before the next performance. Voices could be heard around the scattered tables when Cana and Jeff returned from the dance floor. Cana looked at her friends and cheerfully remarked, "This guy can dance." She looked at Jeff. "I enjoyed that, thank you."

The spotlight followed the next performer hurrying to the stage. The announcer addressed the crowd: "Ladies and gentlemen, give a warm welcome to Hank Sherwood and his Old South Country Band." The crowd roared; several shouted out, "*The Ghost Rider*, let's hear it!"

Hank took the stage holding his guitar and wearing the usual cowboy outfit with a silk neck scarf to boot. The crowd got quiet. Looking out into the dimly lit audience, Hank gave his own introduction. "Thank you, folks. It's a real honor to be here tonight. I'm grateful that you have welcomed my music into your headphones and other such devices that satisfy your taste for country music. Without you folks, I wouldn't be here tonight." Hank paused and turned to the group. "And my lovely wife, Cana Sherwood, is here this evening." As the spotlight turned to Cana, the crowd gave a round of applause. Hank continued, "She stood by me and with me in my career as a songwriter. She is my inspiration for the following tune. And now, she's at the top of my chart. So, this next song is dedicated to Cana, the love of my life." The crowd cheered as Hank Sherwood and the Old Country Band crooned the ballad, *The Tennessee Ghost Rider.*

Cana leaned over and whispered to Lucy, "That smooth lying bastard." She paused. "He makes me sick."

Lucy looked over at Cana. "You're the love of his life, girl. You're at the top of his chart."

"I'm through with his lies, Lucy. I'm not going to listen to another song that comes out of his butt. Lucy, I need to borrow your car for about twenty minutes. I'll be right back."

Lucy took the car keys from her purse and handed them to Cana, then asked, "What's up?"

"I need to drive back to Hank's place and grab something that I left behind. We were in a hurry the other day, and I overlooked it. You guys have fun."

"Okay, Cana." Lucy glanced over at Jeff and then turned back to Cana, "Take your backup with you."

CHAPTER 48

GATEKEEPER: REAL OR UNREAL?

Cana parked in front of her former home; the lights were on inside. When Cana and Jeff reached the front door, they could hear rock music coming from the far side of the house. The front door was unlocked. Cana opened it and yelled, "Anybody home?" She yelled again, except this time louder, "Anybody home?"

"Just a minute," came a voice from down the hall. Momentarily, Hank's girlfriend emerged from the hallway, disheveled looking, wearing nothing but an oversized tee-shirt.

"Oh, what are you doing here?" The girl came face to face with Cana. "Hank's not here."

"I know that. I've come to pick up a portrait, and we'll be gone," said Cana moving toward the bedroom.

"You can't go in there," said the girl.

"Why not?" asked Cana, continuing to walk toward the bedroom.

"Because there's someone in there."

Cana stopped, turned around and replied. "You go in, look on the right side of the closet toward the back and bring me the portrait."

The girl cracked the door open and squeezed in, then closed it. The music stopped. The bedroom door opened and the girl stuck her head out. "You can't have it."

"What!" exclaimed Cana.

"You need to come back when Hank's home."

"I'm not coming back ever! Now, give me my picture or I'm coming in!"

The girl stepped back and opened the door. At the threshold stood a tattooed, shirtless, muscle-bound man in blue jeans. Looking at Jeff in the background, he spoke up. "I'm the gatekeeper, shit head, no one crosses this line."

Jeff stepped up with eyes wide open. "My god, this is déjà vu all over again. I know you."

"Dude, you don't know me. If you don't get the fuck out of here, you will know me."

Jeff slowly took off his coat and shirt and watched as the shirtless gorilla snickered. Jeff moved forward, pushing his foe backward almost to the floor. The man regained his balance and lunged at Jeff. In an instant, Jeff threw him to the floor and commenced pounding him with quick cracking blows to the head.

Cana screamed, "Stop, Jeff. You'll kill him."

Jeff stopped the beating, reached down and pulled the man up by his hair. "Look at me dude." The dazed man looked into Jeff's stern face. "Do you recognize me now?" The man, dazed, shook his head saying, "No, no. Let me up."

"Do you know why you don't recognize me?" Jeff paused and answered his own question. "Because appearance is not reality. Do you remember pulling a guy out of a tree in front of your house about three months ago? That was me, shithead! You put me in the hospital, Mr. personal trainer. I'm not drunk, now! You mosey back to Franklin and tell my *ex*-wife that you ran into the real me." Jeff gave him a final blow that sent him to the floor unconscious. "Cana," he said, "get your shit and let's go."

CHAPTER 49

Living in Crazy

C ana pulled up in front of the Wild Mule Saloon. "I'll circle the block," she said. Jeff got out in his tee shirt and hustled through the front entrance to fetch Leonard and Lucy. Coming back around, Cana spotted the three waiting at the curb. She threw the car in park, hopped out, then yelled to Lucy, "You drive."

Lucy, taking the driver's seat, drove off. Leonard, sitting shotgun, turned to the back seat, "Jeff, what the hell happened, buddy? Did I hear something about the personal trainer?"

"Personal trainer, who is that?" asked Cana.

Jeff chuckled. "The gorilla at the gate is my ex-wife's personal trainer."

"Did you say you kicked his ass?" shouted Leonard.

"I had to pull him off the guy," responded Cana. "Jeff went crazy on his face, made a bloody mess!"

"All good men serve justice," commented Lucy.

"Yes, that's it!" exclaimed Jeff. "My moment of truth!"

"Sure, sounds like you're coming back to life," remarked Leonard. "The old Jeff, the jock at MTSU."

"Let me get this straight," said Cana. "The personal trainer is the boyfriend of Jeff's ex-wife, Betty. He's also the person that put Jeff in the hospital several weeks back. In addition, he's fucking my husband's new girlfriend. What a coincidence!"

"You got it!" snapped Lucy. "Pure tee symmetry, poetry in motion, no coincidence! Congratulations, you two are related by infidelity." Lucy paused for a response, waited, and spoke up. "That was supposed to be funny, guys."

"Lucy," said Leonard. "Your humor is like a pregnant turtle. 'Time hatches the laugh, and no one is around to hear it.'"

"Speak for yourself, Leonard." Leonard grinned and Lucy continued, directing her question to Cana. "You left to pick up something. Did you get what you went for?"

"Yeah, it's here in the back seat, beside me, a portrait of my favorite character."

"I got-ta see this," said Jeff, "Lucy, turn on the overhead a minute." Lucy switched on the light as Cana held the portrait upright for Jeff to see.

"Holy shit!" exclaimed Jeff. "It's Tonto! That's my favorite movie of all time; that's Johnny Depp as Tonto, the Lone Ranger's side kick."

"Who is Johnny Depp?" asked Cana.

"Are you being funny, Cana? Your favorite actor plays the part of Tonto."

"No, Tonto is my favorite character."

"Tonto is the character played by Depp."

"Well, I honor the character over the actor. Tonto is my favorite character."

"Turtle humor all over again," remarked Lucy.

"Whatever," said Jeff. "When that movie came out, I couldn't get over how Disney turned the old Tonto into a shaman. What a touch!" Gazing at the portrait in the light, Jeff went on, "There he is with a dead crow on his head. I

VALIS

liked the image so much that I bought an enlarged print off the internet; it was a digital copy, enlarged. I loved that picture, and my ex-wife hated it. I came in one day, and it was gone. She sold it in a yard sale."

"Really, she sold your print in a yard sale?" asked Cana.

"Yeah, without asking. I couldn't replace it."

"I bought my portrait at a yard sale in Franklin, a year after seeing the movie; it was with my husband, Hank. I loved the movie, and he hated it. This could be the portrait from that yard sale."

"No, this is not the same portrait. Mine was more like a photograph. This is an artistic rendering, far more expressive than the photograph."

"This was originally like a photograph," said Cana. "Hank hated it. So, after rescuing it from the trash, I painted over the image giving Tonto a makeover."

"Well," said Lucy, "you and Jeff share the same taste in art."

"I believe in shamans," said Cana. "One day Tonto spoke to me with his eyes, like in the movie. Hanging on the wall, near the bed, he kept looking down. I got down on the floor and looked under the bed and found used condoms. What I confronted was shock; I knew then that Hank was carrying on an affair while I worked. After that, I kept the portrait out of sight."

"Yeah," said Leonard. "That's interesting, an imaginative message. The simulacrum creates an effect far more reaching than the real. We're living in crazy."

152

CHAPTER 50

THE INTERVIEW

Lucy and Leonard were practicing guitar duets when they heard Jay call out from under the floor. The couple rolled back the kitchen counter and watched Jay pull himself out of the well. "Wouldn't it be easier just to come in the door?" asked Lucy.

"I've been several light years from here, and this well is the short cut back," he replied. Jay shook like a dog and, in an instant, dried himself off. He stepped up on the floor and watched the couple move the portable counter back over the well.

"We need to have a serious talk," said Lucy. "I'm not convinced that we need to go back in."

"I don't have a problem with it," said Leonard.

"That's why we need the debriefing," replied Jay. "So, let's consider where you've been, what you've learned, and what you expect to learn should you choose to return. Let's start with you, Lucy. What have you learned so far?"

"On the first trip into the past, we were watchers, viewing other characters in a Civil War period acting out the drama. We also watched another watcher, a German officer looking in on the same drama. That watcher was remote viewing for the Germans before WWII. These experiences seeped through our everyday life in the form of coincidences – a ghost rider, a side-car motorcycle, running into my best friend, a favorite movie, and a picture meaningfully connected to our friends. Then there was the second trip into the past; we were not watching; we were living in bodies of ancient people; probably lives we've lived before. I was living in the skin of a blind woman. I saw and understood the world in a radically different way when I came out of that girl's skin. The realization was startling. Somehow, she could feel into the souls of others. She could feel – experience – the emotional tension of a crowd gone berserk. She could feel the resentment of the gladiator who reluctantly took her life. Her lived experience was absolutely terrifying. I don't have the proclivity to go back under in the skin of anyone else."

"What about you, Leonard? Tell me what you learned," said Jay.

"Like Lucy, I viewed the Civil War period and watched. We learned from simply watching. We learned about Tom Forrest and chose to believe that he was a good guy. Did I take on a part of his soul? I know this: the aftermath of a soul injection was like being blind and suddenly being able to see. On the next trip into the early Middle Ages, my experience of being in the skin of Alypius, the friend of St. Augustine, was no different than being in my own skin. When I woke up, I could remember and compare differences, even smell him. Saint Augustine and Alypius were converted to Christianity. This conversion was more in line with a serious conviction to live and act in opposition to the circus booths of his age. That, too, bled into what I have lived out in our ordinary world. Saint Augustine heard the sound and verse of children: 'pick up and read.' Jeff and I heard a similar verse on this very spot, 'dig up and read.' I have not had a devastating experience like the blind young woman -- decapitation. Somehow, our friends,

VALIS

Cana and Jeff, are connected to this unfolding, and I'd like to know how it all plays out."

"How it all plays out is important," said Jay. "Augustine was right. You have to start somewhere, and that starting point is authority. You can't do it all alone; you have to trust your teachers to learn. The question is: 'how do you discern a good teacher?' A competent teacher can teach you the craft and art of anything. You can learn the craft of ship-building or the art of war and be successful in both. It's not enough to build a ship; you must be able to sail it. Winning a war is not winning a battle; it is winning the war. Discernment sails the ship; it wins the war; it is not me- centered or man-centered; it is VALIS- centered."

Jay continued, "The booths of St. Augustine's world are no different than the booths of the twenty-first century. VALIS is the mother of all booths, booths within booths, the sum of all information. It is the soul of this information, not the stuff, that calls for discernment. Some human beings only believe in a three-dimensional world; for them there is no soul, no life beyond death, only the atoms and the void. They discern in three dimensions; they think in three dimensions. They choose only to believe in their own personal survival and having an advantage at the expense of any and everything. Everything is a means to an end, their end. They will lie, cheat, and steal to gain an advantage, and it doesn't matter how they look to others. They know that many will buy into their booths of lies. They know that those who know the difference are also seeking to preserve their power. This is the booth of death, that foggy middle region where lost souls fail to cross over into a land of promise; the booth of death is a dark region that enfolds back to the booths of this world."

"But this world is not bad," said Lucy.

"No, certainly not," replied Jay. "This world is in need of attention and care. Discernment, itself, participates in the nature of all souls. The nature of discernment is more virtual

155

than the real or substantial. When the imagination fails, so does the ability to discern. Imagination carries souls into an open-ended future. The failure of imagination carries souls into the cycle of birth and death, a paradox constantly gaining the world, but losing the soul."

"Maybe imagination comes with different pay grades," remarked Leonard, "like IQ points."

Jay cocked his head with interest.

Leonard burst out laughing. "I'm just kidding."

"No, no!" objected Jay. "Keep the image alive. Don't kill the image!"

"Imagination is like a muscle," said Lucy. "You take it to the gym and pump it up."

"It has muscle memory," said Leonard.

"Yeah," said Lucy, "like hitting licks on a guitar."

"And the habit of brushing your teeth in the morning carries you through the day knowing that you're not tasting bad breath," said Leonard.

"That's what I'm talking about guys, imagining your way into and through VALIS."

"What about gathering information before trying to imagine where it might take us?" asked Lucy.

"So, gather the information and see where it takes you, Lucy," replied Jay.

Leonard says he is going back in; I have expressed my doubts because the experience for me was not pleasant."

"Then you learned something," said Jay. "Death can be very traumatic, and human beings can be cruel and insensitive."

"That being said, I want the choice of when I go back in and who I choose to be," replied Lucy. "I don't want to be in the skin of a blind, frightened stranger or at the mercy of a crowd. That's not the kind of life I imagine living through."

"Lucy, you haven't merely imagined a tragic end; you've lived through it in the skin of a blind stranger," said Jay.

"You've already done that! Obviously, you don't want a retake of the same drama. There's no exit from the cross, Lucy. You've always got to be vigilant, aware of the curve ball, so where do you go next?"

"My review of the Middle Ages has brought me to the end of the fifth century and the beginning of the sixth," said Lucy. "I want to visit Boethius, the innocent Christian philosopher, on death row the night before and up until his execution. I do not want to return as Lady Philosophy, the beautiful phantasy physician who took Boethius on a journey into wisdom. That wisdom has been set down in writings of the condemned man. I want to learn if there is something that Boethius is not telling his readers. Also, I wonder how this prisoner faces his execution. Is Boethius really convinced by what he has written in his *Consolation of Philosophy*? How does the *Consolation* affect Boethius' demise? I want to appear as a beautiful woman who is a witness to his execution. I want to discover the weight of his conviction concerning the substance of his imaginings. Was his consolation really mental masturbation?"

"How could you know his lived experience without being in his skin?" asked Jay. "You could be a witness to the execution and still not be convinced."

"Because Leonard is going in under the skin of Boethius, and I would believe Leonard's testimony. There's no reason for Leonard to adopt lies 1600 years later."

Leonard spoke up. "I'm good to go."

"I'm assuming that you both are going back in then," said Jay, "but you should know that there comes a time when the training wheels will come off. You both will have to pick that time. If not, that time may come with devastating consequences."

"Devastating consequences?" questioned Lucy.

"Yes," replied Jay. "The crystal and portal you two are sleeping over opens up your energy field, meaning you vibrate at a higher frequency; you have access to information that gives you power over others. That power is intoxicating and can be misused, the training wheels become a crutch. Forrest used the crystal to keep the South in power; Rommel used it to advance the vision of a madman. It all led to their demise."

"We don't plan to misuse this power," said Leonard. "Surely, we know the difference."

"The crystal is a crutch, Leonard. The real power is within you."

Jay turned to Lucy. "Lucy, Jesus Himself said it, 'the kingdom of God is in you.' Likewise, Buddhism and Hinduism are examples of ancient traditions that awaken you to higher frequencies. When you seek this divine kingdom, you follow the path of righteousness, not from the outside in -- using a prop -- but from the inside out. Working from the inside out, affirms all sentient beings and resonates with the totality of all that is. To do this you have to own and affirm your own existence and grow into this way of being and knowing."

"It can't be bought at any price," said Lucy.

"No, it can't," replied Jay. "It is that treasure hidden in a field that a man finds and sells all that he has to acquire that field. It is the field that you and Lucy have talked about. The treasure is a state of mind where one lives in peace and harmony with all that is. The field is like a quantum field; it has 'no certain dwelling place'; it is 'not made with human hands.'"

"When do we go off the training wheels? Can you give us a hint?" asked Leonard.

"You'll know when," said Jay. "Hopefully, you'll have the conviction to move beyond your vocabulary and be transformed. Learn from the crystal's power before it becomes a burden. Go back in and see what it's like to die a brutal death. Let Lucy find out who this Boethius really is. Come back with information, and use that information wisely."

CHAPTER 51

THE DEATH OF BOETHIUS: DIVINE INFUSION

Jay turned to Lucy with a note of concern. "You guys are going back some 1600 years. Are you sure about going back in?"

"Yes," replied Leonard.

"I'm not asking you, Leonard," said Jay, continuing to gaze at Lucy.

Lucy nodded a yes.

"Lucy, I'm going to be at your bedside on this one," said Jay. "Leonard is your target. I'll let you know when he attains deep sleep, and you can get in bed beside him. When you wake up, you'll be beside a ragged looking man. He won't look anything like Leonard."

When Lucy woke up, she found herself beside a sleeping man on a cot. It was dark, and she couldn't see his face. "Boethius, Boethius," she said, and nudged his shoulder. Boethius turned over and sat up. Lucy stepped back as Boethius turned and sat up on the side of the cot. As he looked into Lucy's shadow, white light began to filter into his prison cell until it filled the room.

Boethius smiled. "Yes!" he exclaimed, "I've been expecting you, my dear."

"You've been expecting me," questioned Lucy. "How can that be? I don't come from your time zone."

"Then what I've written down at the hour of my death is sound," said Boethius. "God's life is not successive like ours. God is an eternal presence. 'Eternity is the complete and perfect possession of illimitable life all at once'."

"I've read that in your work," said Lucy.

"And now, I have assurance that I have been infused with His grace." Boethius paused and looked Lucy over. He smiled, then grimaced. "My, you are one beautiful young woman, even as beautiful as my recent experience of Lady Philosophy."

Lucy looked down at herself and found that she had come to Boethius in the black suit that she worked out in. She could not entirely see herself, and did not recognize the long dark flowing hair falling over her shoulders. "In my time," said Lucy, "Your Lady Philosophy is a memorable character. Your book communicates her beauty. Why don't you refer to me not as Lady Philosophy, but as Lady Theology?"

"Yes, perfect!" exclaimed Boethius. "Lady Theology, you've made my day! Come closer and sit by my side."

"No, I stink," said Lucy. "I've come in my gym suit."

"Hell, this whole place stinks," said Boethius. "You're standing right by my chamber pot." He then stood up and moved the bucket to the far side of his cell. Upon returning to his cot, he sat down and motioned for his visitor to sit down by his side. Lucy sat down by his side and gave Boethius a gentle hug. "I don't know if it would be right to touch such beauty," he said.

"It's all right," replied Lucy.

Boethius gently touched Lucy's face and felt her hair. He moved his hands along her arms. Lucy flexed her muscles. Boethius smiled and looked into her eyes. "It is so very real," he said.

"I've come into your future; your future is my past, Boethius. My year is 2021. I've departed from my living body and traveled back in time. In eternity all of reality has a fictive nature. We refer to it as *virtual reality*. Here I am in what looks like the flesh; it is so real that it instantiates the real."

"Look down at the letters sown onto your outer garment, Lady Theology. In gold letters are the Greek letters *pi* and *theta*. Those letters are the same letters that Lady Philosophy wore on her clothing. *Pi* stands for the practical, as in the philosophy of Aristotle. *Theta* stands for the theoretical, which lies in the metaphysical domain of Plato. Neither approach can be ignored."

"You've admitted to me that you are a Christian, Boethius. Why then, in the last moment of your life, do you turn to Plato and Aristotle rather than Jesus Christ?"

"Philosophy is a preparation for death," said Boethius. "The horse comes before the cart. Philosophy teaches the basics, the idea of how to strive for goodness; virtue is the beginning of Greek wisdom; it teaches us how to live."

"I thought that fear of the Lord was the beginning of wisdom," said Lucy.

"Oh, it is," replied Boethius, "but most of the pagans that I've lived with do not fear the Lord. They fear death. Fear blocks the ability to discern right from wrong and act appropriately. Most people haven't taken a leap of faith into the second birth; they reject metaphysics. The man I faithfully served for many years, King Theodoric of the Ostrogoths, believed only in his five senses. He hasn't learned to live beyond fear; it motivates his every move, deeper and deeper into self-deception and murder."

"It's no different in my time period," said Lucy. "The time that I live in may be worse. People ask the same question that you asked in the *Consolation*: 'why do bad things happen to good people?' Why would a God with divine foreknowledge allow people freedom of choice and then allow them to fall by the wayside? Many throw up their hands when it comes to the affirmation of metaphysics. Metaphysics is not based on the five senses."

"I, Boethius, came to the pagans using what they understood, the five senses. And then, I threw the bomb, metaphysics. God's life is not successive like ours. God is an eternal presence. As I've stated, eternity is 'the complete and perfect possession of illimitable life all at once'." Boethius paused in thought and continued. "God is personally present because I am in prison, and you are paying me a visit."

"What?" said Lucy. "How can you compare me to God?"

"Didn't Jesus say that what you've done for the least of these, you've done it to me?"

"That's true. I came to visit you in prison with my own design. I had read your book and wanted to know first-hand if you were for real, and if you were prepared for death."

"Frankly, my dear, if you had not appeared I would have faced my death in a state of unknowing, but not without faith." Boethius paused in thought and quoted the Christ: 'Blessed are those who have not seen and believe'."

"I hate to tell you this, Boethius, but my coming to you may not be a miracle."

"Oh, why not? Is a miracle necessary for belief?"

"In my time, technology has grown beyond what most of us are able to grasp. We know now that the earth is round. On one side of the earth, a man looks into something like a mirror and sees a town on the other side of the earth. He sees it through the eyes of a man-made flying bird that hovers over that town. This bird is capable of destroying that town with fire simply by automatically responding to a remote viewer's command. What looks like a miracle or magic to you is not experienced that way with me. You see, I have the means to leave my body and travel back in time and experience you with remote viewing and find out for myself."

"You have the means to travel here, but that technology is so advanced that most in your time don't understand it. Is that correct?"

"Yes," said Lucy, "that is correct."

"That doesn't surprise me; it sounds like the workings of someone like Archimedes. Do most people in your time leave their bodies and check out things at a distance?"

"Not many." replied Lucy. "The military uses it to look in on their adversaries. It is acquired through training and practice. Some are born with psychic abilities. I am neither. My means comes through a crystal that stores information. This crystal could be referred to as an *illimitable living information bank*. My spirit guide associates it with VALIS. I don't know whether I am reading the text or the text is reading me. Whatever the case, I'm with you now."

"Did this spirit guide direct you to me?"

"No, I made the choice, and my fiancée, Leonard, is infused with your present experience. Our spirit guide is nearby."

"Oh, I see," said Boethius. "Well then, you've come across power. What you do with that power could have unintended consequences. Surely, Lady Theology has taken that into consideration."

"I have, and I've questioned doing this," said Lucy.

"I can tell you this, Lady Theology. Power is a gift, not delegated without purpose. You can't hide it under a bush; power must be used responsibly and in fear and trembling."

"In my day and time, there aren't many who buy into remote viewing across time. I would say that most people would think that I'm crazy if I told them that I visited a character who lived sixteen hundred years ago."

Boethius grinned. "Perhaps this is a very vivid dream; it's like the real thing, talking to a beautiful young woman whom I can touch. What you call remote viewing could be used for the good. It could be used to prevent killing and destruction. It was my lack of discernment that brought me to this point. I misjudged King Theodoric. I 'fess up to this mistake. Don't take your means of power for granted. Your power has helped bring me to peace."

"King Theodoric did not take your soul, Boethius."

"No, but I misjudged him. If I used what you call remote viewing, perhaps I would not be facing death. On the other hand, if my book is what you say it is, then maybe this is my destiny, something that I must live through and affirm in light of human despair." Boethius paused to collect his thoughts and continued. "I took my learning, wealth, and privilege for granted and shouldn't have. When I was arrested, I felt like an orphan, but God did not intend for me to remain one. My foe taught me a lesson. Pythagorean teachings tell us that we live in a three-dimensional world. In that world you have the choice between good or evil on the horizontal plane. If you choose to live in the house of God, you have to choose righteousness. The last degree of freedom is to act on it, and that move is vertical. Your thoughts, emotions, and actions will not come back empty."

"And your work, inspired by your experience, will not come back empty. You have no idea what an influence your book has had on Western Civilization. If it is any comfort to you, Boethius, your work has endured the test of time. You have encouraged many along life's way. You are truly remembered."

"That's good to know, my dear friend. I suspect that we'll meet again." Boethius looked toward the door. "I can hear them coming for me. Would you be so kind as to be with me until the end?" Boethius took a breath and looked into Lucy's tear-filled eyes then asked, "What is your name?"

"My name is Lucy."

"Lucy, thank you for bringing me to this moment of wonderous being."

The two embraced as the cell door opened. In walked King Theodoric accompanied by two jailers. They could not see Lady Theology standing by the condemned man's side. Theodoric uttered two words: "It's time." Boethius was then ordered out of the cell and into the corridor. A man appeared wearing a mask and ordered Boethius to drop to his knees on the stone floor. The executioner took a cord and wrapped it around the condemned man's temple and eyes. King Theodoric gave a nod, and the executioner began to tighten the cord until the eyes of Boethius popped out of their sockets. As blood ran to the stone floor, Boethius spoke the final words of Christ: "Forgive them, Father, for they know not what they do." King Theodoric gave another nod. The executioner picked up an iron rod and began to club Boethius to his death. Lucy walked back into the prison cell and looked over at the bench and writing desk where Boethius had penned *The Consolation of Philosophy*. On the table was the abandoned manuscript. She turned the pages and read:

> *Happy is he who can see,*
> *Who perceives the clear source of the Good,*
> *Happy is he who loosens the bonds,*
> *Who slips the prison of earth.*[1]

---

[1] Boethius, *The Consolation of Philosophy*, edited and trans. Scott Goins and Barbara H. Wyman (Ignatius Press, San Francisco, 2912), p. 106.

CHAPTER 52

FEDERAL AGENTS ON THE SCENE

The following morning Cana heard a knock at the front door of the Airstream. She peeped out the window and saw two men standing out front. They were wearing white shirts and neckties, with what appeared to be identification badges hanging around their necks. Looking toward the road, she saw a swarm of police vehicles carrying heavily armed men dressed in military gear. When Cana opened the door, she could hear Herk barking in the distance.

"Are you Mrs. Cana Sherwood?" asked one of the men looking up at her.

"Yes, I am. May I help you?" Cana stepped down from the Airstream and stood facing the two men.

"What's going on?"

Politely, the man spoke up, "I'm Federal Agent Hickerson, and this is Agent Cook. We're out of the Columbia office. We'd like to ask you a few questions." Cana gave no reply and waited for the first question.

"We're looking for the owner of this property, a Mr. Leonard Peters. Is he here?"

"He and my friend, Lucy, aren't here. They stay in a cabin further back in these woods. They should be here shortly."

"We're also looking for Hank Sherwood. The record indicates that he is your husband. Do you know his whereabouts?"

"No, sir," said Cana. "I've got a restraining order against him." Hearing the bark of the dog, the group turned to see Leonard emerging from the wooded area. Hurriedly, Leonard made his way to the group.

"Are you Mr. Peters?" asked Agent Hickerson.

"Yes, I am. What's up?"

Agent Hickerson introduced his partner and pointed to the party situated at the edge of the property. "We have a warrant to search the area, including your dwellings."

"What for?"

"It's in connection with the Insurrection on January 6th."

"I'll need to rouse my fiancée," said Leonard. "She's sleeping. She'll need to get dressed."

Agent Hickerson turned to Agent Cook and nodded and then addressed Leonard. "Agent Cook will follow you to your cabin."

Agent Hickerson presented the warrant and motioned for the others to commence the search. "We'll start here," said Hickerson, moving to enter the Airstream.

Cana looked at Leonard. "I'll stay here."

When Leonard, the agent, and several others reached the cabin, the agent tried to enter with Leonard. Leonard, stopped, preventing him from entering.

"Do you mind?" asked Leonard, looking directly into the agent's eyes. "Give me a minute, please."

"You've got five minutes," said agent Cook, stepping back. Leonard closed and locked the door behind him. Lucy kept the blinds closed at night. No one could see in. She had been awake and dressed.

"What's going on?" she asked.

"Help me move this counter, Lucy, no time to explain." The two quickly rolled the kitchen counter aside and peered down at the crystal positioned over the well. Leonard jumped down off the floor and called for Lucy to do likewise. Leonard took hold of one end of the crystal, looked over at Lucy and said, "Let's get it in the well."

"What?"

"Just do it. There's a federal agent at the door, and he's coming in."

After tossing the crystal into the well, the two quickly stepped up to floor level and hurriedly repositioned the kitchen counter over the well area. Thereupon, the agent pounded on the door and shouted out, "Open up or we're coming in." Leonard opened the door, and the men scurried into the room, and the search began.

It took no time for the search party to discover that the kitchen counter was on wheels. As they rolled the counter away from over the opening, Agent Cook walked over and looked down into the well. Turning to Leonard with a wide grin, he expressed admiration, "Man, this is cool -- a cabin built right over your water supply."

"Yeah," said Leonard, "and right under our kitchen."

"Where is your bath, Mr. Peters?"

"Outside for right now. We'll have a compost toilet soon."

"Cool, man, cool, this is a dream home."

As the search team moved out of the cabin, Cana and Agent Hickerson arrived. He, too, strolled over to the well area and looked in. He showed no wonder or surprise, but turned back to Cana. "We need to ask you a few more questions, Mrs. Sherwood." Cana waited for Agent Hickerson to continue. "When was the last time you saw your husband?"

"Last Monday, he was stalking me. My friend Lucy and I were buying groceries in Spring Hill, and he accosted me in the parking lot – wanted me to take him back. I said 'no' and he refused to take 'no' for an answer. He grabbed me and tried to pull me away."

"That's when I stepped in," Lucy interjected, "and neutralized the situation. Hank left, and we proceeded to Franklin to get a restraining order."

"Mrs. Sherwood, do you know that your husband was a part of the mob that stormed the Capitol on January 6th?"

"I knew that he drove to Washington with two others," said Cana. "They were supposed to meet up with others in their group. When I saw the riot on TV, it frightened me; I called Hank. He said that he wasn't a part of it. Later, when he returned to Nashville, he wouldn't talk about it. He became very hostile. Our marriage wasn't working; we broke up."

Agent Hickerson opened up the iPad he was carrying and then turned it on. "I want you to look at this video, Mrs. Sherwood." Cana moved to the agent's side and looked at the screen. She saw the actions of a mob storming the Capitol doors. The agent paused the video and pointed to a figure pushing against the Capitol police.

"Is that your husband, Mrs. Sherwood?"

Cana nodded her head, "So he was there, breaking into the Capitol building. It is unmistakably him. He lied to me."

Agent Hickerson rolled the video forward and, again, pointed to the screen.

"See those two persons, Mrs. Sherwood. Do you recognize them?"

"Yes," said Cana. "I recognize them as being friends of Hank."

Lucy, who was also looking at the screen, spoke up. "I recognize the girl with the orange hair. I met her when I took Cana to pick up her things. She told me that she works on Charlotte Avenue making prosthetics."

VALIS

"Her name is Lisa Bennet," said Agent Hickerson. "Her partner is John Henderson. He manages a private gym in Franklin."

The agent pulled up another video file. This file showed an individual placing pipe bombs in the area. "Do you recognize this person, Mrs. Sherwood?"

"No, because I can't see the person's face."

"You returned to your home on a Friday evening two weeks ago. Do you remember that, Mrs. Sherwood?"

"Yes, I do."

The agent smiled. Evidently, you came prepared, Mrs. Sherwood. John Henderson is a former marine and sniper scout. Henderson is one dangerous dude with a criminal history. Evidently, he met his match. We picked him up at the hospital."

Agent Hickerson withdrew a business card from his wallet and handed it to Cana. "If you hear from your husband, please give us a call." He turned to Leonard. "Mr. Peters, thank you for your cooperation. You folks have a nice day."

CHAPTER 53

Soul Infusion

Leonard opened his eyes and lay still for several minutes. Lucy and Jay looked over from the kitchen table as Leonard rose from the bed. All was quiet in the room as Leonard stood up and made his way to a nearby basin. He dipped in his hands and splashed his face, dried them with a towel, then slowly moved to the table and joined the other two.

Leonard looked over at Lucy. "I can still feel the blows and vividly imagine the pain when I remote viewed Boethius."

"So, what's it like to experience your own brutal murder, Leonard?" asked Lucy.

"This man, Boethius, had the wherewithal to overcome his own murder. Once his eyes popped from their sockets, the pain vanished. He was never once afraid. What didn't vanish was something I've never felt. This man had constant love and compassion for everything, even the man who did him in. When Lucy appeared to him, he felt profound gratitude for having seen into a mystery; it was a transforming experience; he thought that it was like what the Apostle Paul experienced on the road to Damascus." Leonard paused as if to gather a memory and went on. "We hear someone sing or create some work of art -- a poem, a painting, an invention

-- and we refer to it as 'having soul'. This man, Boethius, had soul."

"Well, Leonard, what do you want to hear first, the good news or the bad news?" asked Jay.

"It doesn't matter to me," said Leonard. "Despite the pain, the memory that I carry from this experience doesn't include bad news. All things became new under the skin of this man."

"That's true," replied Jay, "because you have a soul you could connect with Boethius. You took on a soul when you merged with Tom, the man who loved the blind woman. It takes soul to feel empathy and compassion for other human beings. Soul recognizes soul. That is good news. Most believe that we all come into the world with a soul, but that's not true. Many come into the world without a soul, and that's the bad news. These beings are humanoid; Phillip Dick called them replicants. They are created by and through humanoids. They look like humans, act like humans, and talk like humans but lack one metaphysical mystery, a soul."

"What do you mean created by and through humanoids?"

"The universe is occupied by different kinds of beings. They used biological technology to manufacture beings who can procreate. These beings have no soul, nor do they believe in soul. Their abilities are extraordinary, but their ability to imagine and participate in the VAST ACTIVE LIVING INTELLIGENT SOUL are nil. When they die, they die, like a machine. These beings believe that awareness is merely an extension of consciousness, a function of the organization of matter. That is, consciousness is epiphenomenal. Machines, through their own devices, are not capable of merging into VALIS."

"I'm curious," questioned Lucy. "We did come into the world with a soul, didn't we?"

172

"Of course," replied Jay, "and your soul evolves in a succession of lives. Neither of you were manufactured. This was, in part, indicated in your remarks to Monteocha; you'd reached the end of your vocabulary and fear kept you from taking your life. Humanoids live in fear; they act out of fear. The presence of soul gave you the courage to experience another person's death. In this case, to experience his love."

"But that's not altogether true," said Leonard. "As I woke up and came to my senses, I had no compassion for the Ostrogoth. I wanted to avenge the injustice that he perpetuated."

"The answer to that," said Jay, "is that your soul is evolving. You don't take away the living memory from Boethius' experience, nor the experience itself. Boethius had grown into a new suit of clothes; you are not there yet. You've merged into a soul. Now you are merging into a thought adjustor or soul guide, Boethius. After that, you merge into the Spirit of Truth, VALIS itself. At that point you no longer need a guide of souls; you walk in the light of pure divine being. You become a guide of souls, leading others to the Spirit of Truth. You do not fear death or of being born again, under any circumstances. Through this Spirit all things are possible, including the love of all sentient beings. Even soulless beings are sentient."

"You're saying that Boethius is a guide of souls?" asked Leonard.

"Yes, he is, even in his death. The *Consolation of Philosophy* guided many souls toward the light. St. Thomas Aquinas mentions him 35 times in the *Summa Theologica*. Dante places Boethius in the *Paradiso*. Chaucer places 'fate and divine providence' in the *Canterbury Tales*, and goes on to translate the *Consolation*. Many others drew from Boethius in the Renaissance, like Shakespeare and Milton. The Christian scholar, C.S. Lewis, notes Boethius in his work *The*

173

Discarded Image. Even today, the image of fortune as a wheel is alive and well."

"Did Boethius have a soul guide?" asked Leonard.

"He had four of them: Socrates, Plato, Aristotle and Jesus."

"Except for Jesus, they were pagans, Jay."

"It doesn't matter. They pointed toward the Truth. Boethius merged with these thought adjusters and took on the Spirit of Truth."

"When you speak of the Spirit of Truth, I experienced what Boethius understood as the Holy Spirit," said Leonard. "Boethius had encountered what he described as a 'complete and perfect possession of illimitable life all at once'."

"And that encounter was with VALIS," replied Jay, "just another way of expressing it. The Holy Spirit informs or teaches; it reconciles the infinite with the finite; in modern terms, it fuses the quantum level with the visible world of sensible things in time and space in a multiverse where all things are possible."

"Tell me, Jay," asked Lucy, "are you my soul guide?"

"Yes, I am, Lucy. Soon I'll have to go, leaving you with the option to take on a higher power, the Holy Spirit."

"How can it be an option?" asked Lucy.

"Because a choice is an option. I would recommend going into another time, without being under the influence of anyone else. Make the target to be living souls from an alternate universe. Have a chat with them, see what they have to offer, and ask for wisdom. The choice is yours."

CHAPTER 54

HUMAN OR HUMANOID?

Lucy and Leonard spent the next day alone reviewing what had recently transpired. Lucy asked, "Do you regret going back into the life of Boethius and living through his demise?"

"No, not at all," said Leonard. "I downloaded his emotions and thoughts, and somehow realized that these mental images were not of my own making; they were like strangers or objects that pop up as you walk down a crowded street, something you've never seen before. At the moment of his death, Boethius had an insight that brought him to a whole new level of awareness."

"Really," said Lucy, "and what was that?"

"He suddenly realized that the Ostrogoth was a soulless humanoid. Boethius had assumed that Theodoric was educable when, in fact, he had only the capacity to be trained. He did not appear to harbor a sixth or seventh sense. Boethius saw the futility of what he had been up against. He was dealing with a man who lacked vocabulary or imagination. Then Boethius was infused with another thought. He thought about the Spirit of Christ who loved all living beings, even those without souls. He was not afraid to die for them, die in the sense of helping them to act on righteousness."

"Well, you've answered my question, Leonard. Boethius was the real McCoy. He believed in order that he could receive understanding."

"Yes, Lucy. He was the 'real McCoy'."

"Do you want to go back in?" asked Lucy.

"You mean, under someone else's skin? I don't think so. How about you?"

"No. I found it interesting that, despite being in the midst of filth, Boethius had a rather pleasant smell. When we walked out the cell and into the presence of the Ostrogoth and his cronies, the smell was horrid. I don't want to live in the presence of humanoids and stench. I want to learn how to live in my own skin, Leonard. I just want what's right in order to abide in my body. You are a sacred part of my body, and you are music to my soul."

Leonard smiled. "I can go for that. What about exploration? Are you curious to learn more about our universe? Do you believe in some mysterious divine spark that sets real life in motion? Do you believe that we come into the world with a choice: to be human or something much less?"

"Yes, I believe that God created humans in His image; we have a choice, but start out not knowing our potential. In that sense, we're like humanoids. I don't want to die not knowing that I am no more than a machine. I want to explore, take baby steps into the unknown and not be afraid to do so."

"Do you remember the movie, *Blade Runner*?" asked Leonard, and continued. "It was loosely based on Phillip Dick's book, *Do Androids Dream of Electric Sheep?* Harrison Ford played the part of a blade runner. I know this: I don't want to be a blade runner. I don't want to gun down humans or humanoids."

"Yeah," said Lucy. "There's no peace in killing."

"We dropped the training wheels down the well, Lucy. It looks like we'll have to wait and see what happens."

"Yes, and that's where we should leave it," replied Lucy. "Building on what Jay said, I suspect that androids have an undeveloped nervous system, something that technology has yet to develop. I prefer to leave the perfection of an android to God. Whether human souls or machines, these creatures stay in a 'fear or flight' state of mind; they are selfish and will do anything to survive. I don't want to be drawn into this modality; it is contagious and reaps death and destruction. I want to live my life out with you, without the magic of training wheels. I want to live in our own moment, under our own skin, knowing that we contain God's peace which is a way of knowing and being that carries us to His event horizon where we are surrounded by wonderous light."

CHAPTER 55

Don't follow stupid

Dark was beginning to fall when Leonard and Lucy relaxed on the bed and closed their eyes. Their target was non-specific: it came from their imaginings. An alien presence could come forth as anything from a color to an apparition. When nothing happened, the two climbed out of bed. Leonard looked at his wrist watch. It was 10 o'clock when colored lights began to blink behind the curtains covering the windows. The couple could not be sure if they were having a PSI (perfect sight integration) while remote viewing or if they were actually awake in the cabin. Whatever was happening, they walked outside and headed in the direction of the lights. As the path turned to the right, they saw a saucer-like craft about the size of their cabin in an open space. They were drawn telepathically to this craft and were invited up a set of stairs leading to a foyer. They were greeted by an attractive-looking couple, a man and a woman dressed in blue and white uniforms. The couple smiled and informally introduced themselves as George and Harriet. Lucy and Leonard followed them to a sitting room where chairs were placed around a glass-like floor. They were invited to have a seat and were offered refreshments. An attendant entered the room with a bowl of ambrosia and a pitcher of an elixir which she set on a nearby table and departed. Through the glass-like floor could be seen the ground below the craft. "We want you folks to make yourself at home and enjoy the ride," said Harriet. "No need to buckle your seat belts on this ship."

Suddenly, the ship was hovering over the entire area. Looking through the glass bottom, Leonard and Lucy could see the twinkling lights of houses surrounded by darkness. As they moved higher, they saw the street lights in Franklin, Columbia, and Murfreesboro. Instantly, they moved higher, still without any experience of G-force. There they saw morning coming over the earth. At a greater distance, they beheld the entire living earth, blue in color. The next shot was a view of a full moon. "You've come this far," said George, taking a seat and addressing the couple. "I assume you might want to take a closer look."

Harriet gave a command as if talking into a command system. "Cruise to the moon in appropriate time for human interaction." Harriet poured herself a cup of water and turned to the guests. She smiled, then spoke up, "We've been through this visit with many others over the years. You folks want to know who we are, where we're from, and something about our view on things."

"Yes, that's right," said Lucy.

"Well," said George, "we come from the Pleiades star cluster, about 410 light-years from Earth in the constellation of Taurus. We belong to a galactic federation, and our mission is to humanize the citizens on an evolving earth."

"Let me just start by adding this," said Harriet. "You may think that we're highly advanced entities. That's relative to what you're comparing us to. There may be other civilizations, far older than ours, looking down on us. The fact is that there is more that we don't know than what we do. We know that it is possible to engage in psychic phenomena and that some people have a well-developed extra-sensory perception and some learn it. We've remote viewed everything that you have and more. We've lived long enough to know your questions before you ask them. What we know is what you're trying to understand. The fundamental question is whether or not the physical body survives bodily death. The answer is both yes and no. Humans survive bodily death; humanoids do not. Humans are made in the image of VALIS; humanoids are not. Humans resonate with VALIS while humanoids resonate only with themselves; the former are connected to the universe; the latter are connected only to themselves. They are man-centered, not God-centered. They reflect a narcissistic frame of mind."

Harriet paused and waited for a response. Leonard spoke up. "While under the skin of Boethius, I went out with enormous empathy for the humanoids who took my life. Why?"

"Because that's what makes you human."

"You're saying humanoids can't feel empathy?"

"As far as we know, it works this way," said Harriet. "All creatures are composed of matter. Matter vibrates in many frequencies. We are all energy units. You, Leonard, as an energy unit are capable of resonating on a quantum level. Humanoids were once manufactured to be slaves for our people. This was a mistake. We lacked the technology to produce a self-organizing creature. Humanoids have no pineal gland, a key component in the activation of their energy level. They, these replicants, are indeed energy units, but they have only three energy centers in their bodies, what has been referred to as the lower chakras. Their emotions are real and reflect fight or flight. They experience fear more than anything else and will stop at nothing in order to manifest and preserve themselves. Boethius was a threat to the Ostragoth who took Boethius out doing what he was programed to do. And you, Leonard, experienced the brutal execution."

"Is there no hope for these humanoids?"

"In a quantum universe, all possibilities are on the table, but we know of no mansion world that contains such replicants. We gather that these creatures live in mental torment, that they are incapable of living in peace."

"So," questioned Lucy, "what makes us any different from these replicants or humanoids?"

"Don't take me literally, but think of it this way: you were created to be self-organizing; you came into being by the hand of God. Your body consists of seven energy centers on your spine, three above and three below the heart chakra. There is a ground chakra below your feet and two above your head. You have a pineal gland. With this hardware, the human body can connect to what has been described as a divine level."

Lucy asked, "Are you saying that these replicants lack higher energy centers, but are close copies of humans?"

"Yes, I am. They are so close in appearance that it is difficult to weed them out or distinguish them from humans. The New Testament speaks of this in The Parable of the Wheat and the Tares; you have to wait on the harvest for the wheat and tares to be separated. You see, humans come into the world with the lower chakras fully operational; those base energy centers are where the undeveloped soul learns to live. Generally, almost without exception, learning to live precedes ascending to a metaphysical level. That's why we don't try to separate the sheep from the goats. We might say, we're simply watching. Mostly we watch the circulation of souls in a movement of death and rebirth. Take the Civil War, for example, the North won the war, but the conflict still exists; tribalism remains in the active memory of a population of undeveloped souls. People are born into a world that clings to the past. They repeat the same old habits and patterns."

"So, what would be your advice to us?" asked Leonard.

"You have to step out of the crowd," said Harriet. "You have to die to the ways of this world. To do this you have to love all things. You have to move beyond past bad habits and oppressive memories. In this epoch, it's the Civil War. You can't do that through strife or division. The beginning of your journey begins with changing yourself, not the other guy. To engage the humanoid will surely lead to a perpetual reoccurrence of your past. As for you, Leonard, unless you drop your biases, you will return to the end of your vocabulary. There is a Buddhist saying about a turbulent muddy pond that reflects nothing. When this pond is still, it reflects the moon perfectly. You have to be still and clear your mind."

"I discovered a crystal, a few months back," said Leonard, "seemingly by accident. I heard the words, 'dig up and read.' I remote viewed Augustine's conversion after he heard an unusual message: 'pick up and read.' Now, was that merely a coincidence?"

"Crystals store information. Like your people, we use crystals in technology. In a self-organizing universe with holographic properties, such occurrences are considered a definitive probability," said Harriett.

"We humans die, but do your people ever die?" asked Lucy.

"Let me put it to you this way," said George. "I've lived over a thousand years. Harriet and I chose to return as physical beings. We're here for people like you. Every part of my body has been replaced, except for my brain. However, my brain is not my mind; it is a sense organ that connects me to a vast information network, the Akashic Records. We are essentially spiritual beings having a physical experience. The brain and even the heart act as transducers, changing one form of information into another. The mind and the heart are not something that can be manufactured. There appears to be a power greater than the sum of all its parts."

"So, you're telling us that your people have the technology to make all body parts except a mind?" asked Lucy.

"Oh," said George. "We can grow a brain and a heart; we can make a sentient being. But the mind is not in the brain, and neither is the heart a piece of meat. Technology can give me another brain, but what comes out is nothing like the coherent me. Even with a download of my memories, something is missing: curiosity and imagination. It's something like a ship going to sea with a carpenter on board. Over the years the ship begins to fall apart, and the carpenter replaces the ship board by board. In time, it is not the same ship; its personality is lost. It's not the original. In our case, the personality remains, and we have not cracked that mystery."

"So, you're not willing to take on another brain, one that is alien-made and downloaded with all of your memories?" asked Leonard.

"Hell no," said George. "Manufacturing an adaptive creature -- one that maintains an identity and is open to the future -- is not something that is possible in our mansion world."

"I agree," said Harriett. She then spoke through the command system: "please release the video monitor."

From the opposite side of the room, across from the glass viewing port, a huge video monitor emerged from the wall. George picked up a remote control and turned it on. Lucy and Leonard looked up to see a video of the January 6th attempt to overthrow the American government and the rule of Law. Harriet and George were displaying a mob staging an insurrection.

George stood up and shook his finger at the screen. "That's what I'm talking about," he said. "A wondrous experience in democracy gone amuck, and we have created a monster with our own vain imaginings."

"I'm not clear what you mean," said Leonard. "Who created what?"

"Most of that mob are replicant slaves created by us thousands of years ago. They have multiplied like viruses."

"Let me guess," said Lucy. "The mob consists of two types of sentient beings, replicant slaves and normal human beings who are so much alike that they cannot be sorted out."

"That's right," replied Harriet.

"Surely, there's got to be a way of sorting them out," remarked Leonard.

"The difficulty," said Harriet, "comes when people are slaving so hard at survival that they have no time to sit back and take account of their situation. Some are downright lazy, and some are just plain stupid. We manufactured the stupid type. They are dead set to slave for survival out of fear. Let one of them take charge, and he will become their cult leader. Oppressed humanoids naturally follow the crowd, looking for the tyranny of a messiah. This false prophet or false messiah fails in imagination. His imagination is self-centered; it goes no further than himself. His imagination fails to connect with the life world of others. The lazy are out for a free ride; they fall in line with the messiah's one-sided imagination."

"So, you guys threw a monkey wrench into civilization thousands of years ago," said Lucy.

"Yes, we did," said Harriet. "We messed up. That's why we have a general policy of being distant from these creatures. We watch while humanoids serve their own interest, as in their questionable use of dangerous technology. Take the Fukushima Daiichi nuclear disaster in 2011 and the Chernobyl disaster in 1986. These are examples of dubious intentions in purely materialistic programming. With humanoids, it doesn't matter who is watching or how stupid they look to others; they will lie, cheat, and steal to accomplish what they perceive to be their advantage."

"Do you hold out hope for these people?" asked Lucy.

George answered the question. "There may be hope for the hard-working and the lazy to be liberated from the prison of oppression. As for manufactured humanoids, the mother of all blunders, I personally have my doubts. All of these creatures seem not to be able to develop a personal ethic or practical reason or habits that require an ability to delay personal gratification, but that, in itself, is not enough. How do you turn a dog into a god other than swapping the letters?"

"So," said Lucy, "let me sum up what I'm hearing. We're taken up by friendly space aliens, on our way to the moon, and I am told that you folks make mistakes, possibly a mistake that prevents the establishment of life, liberty, and the pursuit of happiness for its citizens. These creatures that you're watching appear to have some sort of death instinct. If they had your technology, they would misuse it, even turn it on themselves."

"It could come down to mutual self-destruction," said Harriet.

"Or apocalypse," said George.

"I hope the prophets are right," said Harriet. 'Love or die'."

"But I can't tell you that any one faith group has a franchise on truth," said George, "but they all tend to have a common thread of peace and good will. We are constantly looking beyond ourselves. Our Federation recognizes our dependence on an open-ended universe. We move into an unknown future in a posture of fear and trembling. At the same time, we have hope and are optimistic."

The space craft reached the moon. The guests and their hosts looked through a glass portal as they moved past rocks and craters. On the dark side of the moon, Lucy and Leonard beheld what looked to be a space station. There were other space craft moving around. Within seconds their ship landed back at the point of departure. Harriet escorted the couple to the foyer that lead to the exit. As they moved, Harriet placed her hand on the right side of Lucy's back. Lucy felt her warm touch and looked into Harriet's face.

"Lucy, you'll be fine."

"Thank you," said Lucy. She hesitated, as if wanting to say something.

"Just love one another," said Harriet. "Work for a living and enjoy what you do. Help others when you can. Above all, don't follow stupid."

CHAPTER 56

To KNOW THYSELF

In mid-morning, Lucy and Leonard were roused by the sound of knocking coming from under the kitchen counter. Leonard pulled himself out of bed and rolled back the kitchen counter. Lucy sat up in bed and looked over at the opening. Neither of them were surprised to see Jay step into the room. Who else could it be? However, they were quite surprised to see who followed Jay up into the living area.

The man who stood beside Jay wore a buckskin outfit and a headband. Lucy and Leonard turned their faces to one another and declared, "I know that guy!"

"You sure do, guys," said Jay. "This is none other than Tonto, the soul guide for the Lone Ranger. "

"Well," said Lucy, "he sure doesn't look like Johnny Depp."

"Of course not, Lucy," said Jay. "Johnny is an actor."

"What's he doing here?" asked Leonard.

"He is the spirit guide for Cana and Jeff."

"I don't doubt that," said Lucy. "They both wound up with his portrait."

"He does look like the character in the portrait," said Leonard.

"You guys feel like going back in?" asked Jay.

187

"No," said Lucy. "We had all the drama we can stand."

"How about another shot with the crystal?"

"I thought we were off the training wheels; why are you egging us on to take it back?"

"Good," said Jay. "What are your plans now?"

"A vacation," said Lucy.

"Yes," remarked Leonard. "We're motoring West in the camper."

"We're going to make a living for ourselves," chimed in Lucy.

"You don't need to work," said Jay.

"It's not like work, work," said Lucy. "It's like making music and money at the same time; something that should go hand and hand."

"Leonard looked affectionately at Lucy and added, "We'll find ourselves in a musical event before reaching Mt. Shasta." Leonard looked back at Jay. "What about you, Jay?"

"First," replied Jay, "I'm delighted by the decision that you folks have made. I've racked up enough kingdom points to move on to another mansion world."

"What does that mean?" asked Lucy.

"I was right about you guys that you would make a wise decision."

"The right decision?" questioned Leonard.

"The consensus is that you both made the right decision," replied Jay. "Last year, just before the pandemic, we were on our way to Oregon to see Lawrence."

"Yeah, I remember," said Leonard.

"Surely, you recall my making bets with what you thought were imaginary characters, bets about the future."

"I do."

"I bet big on you guys that neither of you would misuse the crystal. I doubled down on your choice not to continue fighting the Civil War. It became something like a promotion."

"How do you know for sure that we made the right decision?" asked Lucy.

"Because you are in line with the presence of non-contention."

"You mean we're passivists?" asked Leonard.

"Something like overcomers," replied Jay.

Lucy and Leonard turned to each other with a look of surprise. Lucy then turned to Jay. "I remember that word, 'overcomer'. She turned back to Leonard. "When we first met, that word triggered a deep intuition that we were destined to meet."

"Knowing runs deep," replied Jay. "You both are being honest with yourselves. You might say that you have emerged out of the past into a new presence. I'd say that you are at the beginning of a new vocabulary. To 'know thyself' is to confront your limits, the boundaries, that you can and cannot cross. As you are able to discern the babbled images of crowds, you will evolve. You have to know yourself before you can return to the fray and pick out lost sheep. I've got work to do in another mansion world. I'm leaving this *neck of the woods* to my friend Tonto. I'll catch up with you guys later, maybe back in Mt. Shasta."

Turning to Tonto, Lucy asked, "And what's in our *neck of the woods*?"

"Jeff and Cana," replied Tonto. He paused and continued with a question, "How well do you think you know your friends?"

"We all grew up together. Pretty well, I'd say," replied Lucy.

"Do either of you want to make a bet on it?"

"Maybe," interjected Leonard. "Let me ask you a question, Tonto. Have you ever actually met Cana and Jeff, I mean, in the flesh?"

"I've never met anyone in the flesh, Leonard, even you two. I am a copy of an original image. Jeff and Cana have embraced those copies. Justice is what I seek, Kemosabe. The Good always lies behind a mask. I suspect that they, too, will hide behind a mask and seek justice."

"What?" asked Leonard? "What are you talking about?"

"Virtue cannot be taught, Kemosabe!" replied Jay. "Justice lives behind a mask."

"How can goodness possibly live behind a mask?"

"Because, Kemosabe, you can't define it; you can only imagine it. Goodness comes to light when it is lived. This light – the light of the good -- is 'beauty too rich for use, for earth too dear!' Goodness is too good for this world; it's too beautiful to die and be buried."

Cana chuckled and cocked her head. "My, my, a Socratic Shakespeare in the guise of a Native American shaman;" she paused and continued. "We're having our friends over this evening for dinner. You're more than welcome to come, Tonto. I'm sure they will be thrilled to meet you, especially if you come up from the well."

"Indeed," said Tonto, "they will be one step closer to the original."

"And before we head out, I'll leave the keys to this cabin with Jeff," said Leonard. "After all, he found this place, heard a calling, and made it possible for me to return home. I suspect that he and Cana will go into the night, unafraid of the dark, with a taste and vision for justice. I don't know for sure what the outcome will be, but I'll bet that the two of them dare to brave the journey."

THE END

PREVIOUS BOOKS BY
THE AUTHOR

In this book, Chaplain Welborn describes his ministry as one of storytelling. Not only does Welborn share his story, inmates, staff and volunteers share theirs. The reader is taken to "death watch" and the execution chamber where one faces the consequences and mystery of an execution. The author speaks out against capital punishment.

A major theme in these reflections addresses the unexpected within the narrative of a prison community. These uncanny experiences concern the importance of human subjectivity. If glimpsed, such moments can be transforming; they take into account imagination and the power of imagination that drive our choices.

For purchase of the book, go to Amazon.com.

A life review has the makings of a transforming story. A rupture in the narrative puts story into motion; we have the grace that brings life or the negativity that destroys it. Something happens that one does not expect, be it one of great exhilaration, like falling in love, or one of regret and despair, like going to jail. The power of a life review is an awakening to these events for the purpose of moving the narrative forward in a more robust manner. I do believe that each of us is behind the helm of our ongoing story, but we are not the captain of our soul. When the world is hit with a coronavirus, we are carried across a familiar boundary into an unexpected one. The turning point in the story creates the possibility for transformation. Do we continue to treat other people and the environment like objects for our own personal consumption or do we take on a new way of being human? We have no idea of how much is in store for those driven with a divine purpose.

For purchase of the book, go to Amazon.com.

Made in the USA
Middletown, DE
23 May 2023

31018075R00123